Her Second Chance Cowboy

Speculation is out of control and running rampant in Ransom Creek about the new waitress at the Goodnight Café. What's her story?

Libby Smith, aka Libby Dunaway, can't catch a break. She's been on her own since she was seventeen and has struggled but made it, until everything caught up to her... Now, hiding out in the small town she hitchhiked to after the unexpected happened, she's hoping to lay low until it's safe to go home, if ever. Thankfully, the townsfolk are nice and the cowboys too...especially one who totally throws her off every time he walks into the room.

Professional bronc rider Vance Presley is at the top of his profession when he comes home for his brother's wedding and sees the new waitress at the café again. She's cute and nervous when he's around, dropping things and freezing up and totally adorable. Funny thing is, every time she looks at him with those big blue eyes of hers, he can hardly think straight himself.

When she shows up at his brother's wedding, he asks her to dance…and that's when things spin out of control.

Sweet romance is blooming in Ransom Creek, one cowboy at a time. Enjoy a good, clean and wholesome romance series readers are falling in love with!

VANCE:
HER SECOND-CHANCE COWBOY
Cowboys of Ransom Creek, Book Five

DEBRA CLOPTON

Vance: Her Second-Chance Cowboy

Copyright © 2018 Debra Clopton Parks

CHAPTER ONE

Libby Dunaway, known to the town of Ransom Creek as Libby Smith, carried the plates of burgers into the dining room of the Goodnight Café. She had adjusted to keeping her real name a secret and justified using the false name because she must for the time being. She was doing what she had to do and that's all she could do at this point.

Holding the plates of the roast beef special steady, she scanned the diner and almost tripped when she spotted Vance Presley sitting with his brother Drake. Her mouth went dry. He must have come in while she was in the kitchen. Her stomach clenched with instant nerves.

She sucked in a deep breath and tried to calm her emotions.

The bronc rider was about the best-looking man she'd ever seen, and he reminded her so much of her Mark that it was uncanny. And disturbing on so many levels. And had been from the first moment she'd laid eyes on him, not long after she'd hitchhiked to town and taken this job at the café. When he'd walked into the diner the first time and his gaze locked onto hers, she'd thought for a moment it was Mark, back from the dead. She'd almost fainted. She managed not to, but had dropped the burgers she'd been carrying.

His beautiful bright eyes and mischievous, happy look was so reminiscent of Mark that it was a miracle she hadn't hit the floor with the plates.

Now, he was here again and she couldn't think straight.

Get a grip, Libby.

She was trying but her heart pounded and her hands were trembling beneath the plates of Gert's roast beef with gravy and potatoes lunch specials.

I will not drop the plates. I will not drop the plates.

Thankfully the handsome bronc rider wasn't in town that often, but of course he was here this weekend for his brother's wedding.

It wasn't just his resemblance to Mark, but her other unsettling reactions. Because when Vance Presley was around, her thoughts flew to soft kisses and the hope of strong hugs and security. It was unacceptable.

She fought to gain control and forced her eyes off Vance while she concentrated on the shaking plates and managed to calm her trembling hands.

As if drawn to a magnet, her gaze lifted, met his across the room, and locked on him; she couldn't move. He was amazing. More than amazing. He took her breath away and her good sense. She frowned, blinked, and yanked her eyes off the cowboy as guilt slammed into her.

What was wrong with her?

She hadn't been thinking straight since she'd run nearly two months ago and ended up here.

But right now, she needed to not drop these lunch specials.

When she spotted Vance stand up and take a step toward her, she froze. Her hands began to shake uncontrollably.

Not again. Vance grimaced as he saw the plates start to fall. The cute waitress had gone completely white. This was his third trip home from the rodeo circuit since she'd shown up in town and Gert had hired her. Each time he'd entered the café, she'd dropped plates of food. He felt bad because his brothers told him she only did it when he came to the diner. He'd been waiting for her to come out of the kitchen, and when their gazes locked, it was like a wild Mustang had just kicked him in the gut. He stood, drawn to her. He'd known the moment she started trembling it was going to happen again, but he was determined that she didn't drop another plate because of him. He moved toward her. When the plates slipped from her hands, he rushed forward.

The room went silent as three plates of Gert's roast beef and gravy landed in his arms, sloshed over his jeans and came to rest across his Tony Lama boots and clattered to the floor.

His attempt at catching them was a colossal fail.

"Your boots," Libby gasped, her big eyes full of regret. "I am so sorry." Her voice broke.

Fearing she was about to cry in front of the entire lunch crowd, he grinned. "Don't be. I'm a big fan of Gert's roast beef." He plopped a gravy-covered finger into his mouth and then pulled it out clean. "I think I'll be having that for lunch."

Instead of finding him funny, her face crumbled. "But…your expensive boots."

He shot a quick glance at the gator hide boots. "These are work boots. A lot worse than roast beef gets on them when I'm traipsing around in arenas. A little gravy isn't going to hurt them." He felt the overwhelming need to hug her but the gravy he was wearing kept him planted where he was. "Please don't look so horrified. It's okay. I promise."

"But it's everywhere." She yanked a rag from her

back pocket and began wiping gravy off his arms. The instant she touched him, his skin tingled, eclipsing the sting of the hot gravy. He swallowed hard as she looked up into his eyes, her blue eyes so wide with worry that he thought he could get lost in them if he leaned down closer...but he held himself still.

Libby was pretty with her big blue eyes, her pert nose, and soft, upturned lips. He was on the road constantly and around some beautiful women, but he'd never in his entire twenty-five years ever felt the sudden burning desire to know everything there was to know about a woman before he'd met Libby.

He was suddenly wondering how her pretty pink lips would feel against his.

He frowned, and shut down the thought. "It's okay. I'm fine." He covered her hands with his to stop her fussing over him as he realized the whole diner was watching them. He smiled, trying to ease her worry as he gently pried the rag from her fingers. "Libby, really, let me have the cloth and I'll clean this up."

Her hands stilled beneath his and her gaze lifted to

meet his. Vance's world stilled, came into focus...it was almost like the instant he settled in the saddle on a bronc's back, right before the chute opened and the ride began...he lived for that feeling...

"And I'll help clean the floor." Gert saved the day, breaking into the moment as she came from the back with more rags and a mop.

Libby swung around to face the perky café owner. "I am so sorry, I did it again," she half whispered, maybe realizing they were the show of the day.

Gert chuckled and so did several of the café patrons, making Libby pale more.

He shot a glare over his shoulder and the chuckles died down.

"No worries, Libby. It all wipes up." Gert went to work. "Let's get this cleaned up while Romeo there gets *himself* cleaned up. I already told the cook to start that order over. I had a sneaking suspicion you were going to lose it when I saw Vance walk through the door."

Vance wasn't sure whether he should grin at that. His brothers had speculated that Libby had a thing for him. But he wasn't so sure whether it was a thing or whether she was scared of him. Or maybe it was something else. He just knew he wished she didn't start shaking at the sight of him.

"I'll head out back to the faucet."

"Stop at the sink in the kitchen." Gert waved him toward the kitchen. "It will be fine. No need to hang out on my back porch. For one, you might run into the skunk that's been hanging around back there."

"Yikes! I'll do that. I wouldn't want to meet up with a skunk at the moment." He cleaned up while Hoss, the part-time cook, laughed from where he was cooking at the grill.

"That girl can't seem to hold nothin' when you're around. She don't do that with anyone but you. She gets all nervous when Sheriff Reb comes in too, but she ain't dropped anything yet. I'm kinda wondering like the rest of the town if she might be in trouble with the law or something. But if she is, Reb ain't found it out and you ain't the law, so that makes me think she just has a thing for you."

Vance frowned. "I don't know. The way she stares

at me, she could be scared of me for some reason."

"Hardly." The big man shook his head. His face scrunched up with the smile. "She's a real nice kid. But I shor wish I knew her story. Maybe you can find it out. See if she's in some kind of trouble."

Vance finished cleaning up. He had wet spots on his jeans—his shirt, too—but his boots were now clean and he could walk back out and sit down at his table. He was sure he was going to get a lot of teasing from the cowboys who'd witnessed the disaster. They could tease him all they wanted but they'd better leave Libby alone. He had a feeling they wouldn't hurt her feelings. Anyone could see she was clearly upset.

Still, cowboys loved giving each other a hard time and he gave as good as he got, so he could handle it. Something about Libby got him in the center of his chest. If what Hoss was saying was true, then everyone was looking out for her. And wondering the same thing. Cooper's wife, Beth, had said the women were all trying to gain her trust so she would confide in them if she was afraid about something. Or running from someone. She'd told Cooper to get the men to keep their ears and eyes open too.

And they were. Now, he looked at Hoss. "I might just try and do that."

Hoss nodded and slid a burger onto a bun. "Good. I thought you might."

Libby's cheeks burned hot when Vance came back into the diner from the kitchen. People were real nice and didn't tease her about her clumsiness but still, she knew they were thinking about it. And she had a feeling the cowboys would all tease Vance. As much as she tried not to, her getting klutzy when he was around made it seem to everyone that she had a thing for the cute cowboy. She didn't. Feeling a little more in control, she headed to meet him as he strode her way.

"You cleaned up well." She struggled to find the right words instead of those cascading out of her mouth.

"See, I told you a little gravy and beef wouldn't hurt me. Are you okay?" His gaze bore into her, as if searching every hidden corner of her eyes.

She fought to hide her emotions, not wanting anyone to see what lay there in the shadows of her heart, if indeed the eyes were the mirrors of the soul or heart. She managed a halfway normal, "Yes."

"Good, I wanted to make sure. Because I am, just so you know to rest easy."

Rest easy... The man muddled her brain with the swarm of uneasy emotions him being around caused her, much less so close and so focused on her. She had no words; she couldn't even find wrong words to say.

As if understanding, he smiled. "Okay, I'm going to sit down over here and leave you alone. I think Drake already ordered so I'm going to save you a trip to our table by ordering the roast beef lunch special." He winked and strode past her to slide into the booth with his brother.

She headed toward the kitchen and straight to the rear freezer area, where she leaned her forehead against the large stainless-steel door and fought to settle her nerves.

Hoss chuckled, reminding her that she wasn't alone in the kitchen. She looked toward the front, where she could see the big man studying her.

"You look as white as fresh snow right now. You're doing right. Take a few deep breaths and relax." He came her way and patted her on the shoulder. "You're going to have to figure a way to stop nearly fainting when that Presley brother comes through those doors, young lady. Anything I can do to help, you just ask."

He had a small window over the grill so he could see into the café, so obviously he'd witnessed her reaction and read it right that she'd almost fainted. "It's complicated, Hoss, but thank you."

"I'm just letting you know." He turned to head back to the grill.

"Oh, Vance ordered a special," she said and that got another chuckle.

"Well, it's good to know one of you can talk. I'll make a special. Then you can carry it out there and put it on the table in front of him like none of this ever happened. Heck, you might try having a short conversation with him. Like, say, I hope you enjoy this."

She groaned, getting another chuckle from Hoss.

"You can do it. Say something but for heaven's sake, hold on to the plate. Okay?"

"Okay, but it just isn't that easy. My whole insides knot up. And my hands shake. Not to mention the fainting part. It's embarrassing."

"Clearly it's like two stars colliding—like in all them romance books."

Her head jerked back to look at him. *What did Hoss know about romance books?*

He grinned. "Don't judge me just because I like to read a romance every once in a while. Helps me try and figure out what a woman likes." He frowned. "But the thing I don't get is why all the heroes have long lashes. What's that about?"

She laughed. She enjoyed reading and yes, she had also seen the many references often found in the books with the heroes having long lashes. "I'm not sure, but I kind of like the intense eyes myself—not the lashes." Vance's intense eyes flashed before her. Not Mark's.

Hoss turned from where he was dishing up the roast beef. "It's good to hear that laugh from you. You know what I think? You two need to see each other outside the walls of this diner. You can sit and say nothing but maybe get comfortable with this thing sparking between y'all."

She walked to the front. "There's no 'thing' between us. Believe me, he just makes me nervous. Besides that, he can do better than me."

Hoss gave her a sharp look, almost angry. "What do you mean, better than you? Ain't nobody better than anyone else in this world. Nobody. And if somebody thinks they're better than you, then they've got the problem. Vance ain't like that, I can tell you for a fact."

She'd said too much. She'd been upset and talked too much when she'd known better. "I didn't mean it that way. Hand me the plate and I promise not to drop it." He did and she turned away then paused and looked over her shoulder. "Thanks, Hoss, for being so kind."

The big bear of a man with the romantic heart winked at her. "Go get 'em, girl. You've got this."

If he only knew how wrong he was.

CHAPTER TWO

The next day, after much teasing from his brothers, Vance pulled on his Western cut tuxedo jacket. Jenna had asked all the groomsmen to wear their starched blue jeans. He'd been glad of that because he was much more comfortable wearing them rather than a full tuxedo. To top it off, he set his gray Stetson on his head and headed outside to join the family.

He wondered how Libby was today. He kept seeing those beautiful, distressed eyes of hers and all he could think about was making her relax and smile.

"Oh, don't you look handsome," Aunt Trudy

squealed as she hustled up on her short legs and looked him up and down. "You do clean up nice, baby boy."

"I'm not a baby, Aunt Trudy." She loved to tease him and he gave as good as he got. "And may I say that you clean up right nice yourself, young lady."

She puffed up with happiness at the compliment. "Oh, thank you. I've put on a few pounds but I'm still going to have me some cake."

"I'm having some too."

"So," she smiled the familiar smile that told him she was up to something or after something, "I witnessed that cute diner disaster that you and that sweet Libby had yesterday. I just want you to know that we've made sure she got an invitation to the wedding. But she told Gert she didn't feel right coming. So, Gert gave her a bit of a sob story on how she needed extra help watching over the buffet table and she agreed to come help with the catering."

Yup, they were up to something and it smelled like matchmaking of a sort. At the moment he didn't care because he was glad to hear she would be at the wedding.

"Maybe you could make sure she gets to dance a few times."

Oh, he planned on that. "I'd be happy to."

"But while she's around the food, I need you to try to stay clear of her. We don't need a repeat of yesterday at the reception."

He laughed. "I'll hide behind a fern or something. How does that sound?"

"Perfect." She patted his arm and he realized she looked distracted.

"Is everything all right, Aunt T?"

She smiled and glanced toward where the wedding chairs had just been set up a few moments ago. "Fine. Everything is fine. I better go check the extra food in the back. But don't forget about dancing with Libby."

He watched her head inside then started across the yard toward the tents. What his aunt didn't know was wild horses couldn't keep him from asking Libby to dance. Matter of fact, she was the only girl he was going to ask to dance. He thought if he could figure out why she looked so upset and dropped things, then maybe he could help her. Maybe he could stop the plate dropping, too, because he didn't want to stop going to the café when he was in town.

And he wanted to know what her story was. There were rumors running around town and all kinds of speculation going on. He knew she'd shown up with almost nothing to her name and she stayed to herself and had been pretty quiet in the almost two months that she'd been there. She just worked at the diner, got her paycheck, and kept to herself. The gals had said they had invited her to lunch and stuff but she'd never taken them up on their offer.

He wondered whether she had plans to stay. *Or was she just here to get a paycheck, sock it away and then move?* For some reason, that question chewed at his thoughts. He didn't want her to leave. He wanted her to stick around. He was fixin' to have a brief stint at home after his next two rodeos and hoped he could get to know her better. He hadn't felt this much interest in someone in a very long time.

He'd been so focused on winning top award in bronc riding at the National Finals Rodeo in Vegas that he hadn't let himself get involved with a woman. Too much drama and distraction.

He'd barely missed winning two years in a row and this was going to be his year. He just had to stay focused. His brain relived every turn and every buck of his last ride and he was determined that this December in Las Vegas, he was going to have the ride of his life and win the title.

He wasn't giving himself any other option.

But right now, his main goal was to watch Shane and Jenna get married. And then he was going to do a little dancing with a shy waitress, if she'd say yes.

"It looks good, Trudy." Gert slapped her hands on her hips and surveyed the wedding setup as pride filled her. "We did it up nice."

"We did, didn't we?" Trudy sighed from two steps away.

Gert realized rather than a satisfied sigh, her friend was worried. "What's that about? You sound depressed or something. With one more of your nephews getting married, I figured you'd be jumping the moon right about now."

"Gert, the chairs are brown. They're supposed to be white."

"Really?" Gert studied the area she'd just admired. "They look fine. I didn't even notice."

"But they were supposed to be white. That's what Jenna wanted. The truck got lost on its way here and she won't see it until she comes out of that house in forty-five minutes in her wedding dress."

Gert stuffed her hands on her hips and gave her high-strung friend an *are-you-kidding-me* glare. As one of her closest friends, it had always been her and Sally Ann's job to talk high-strung Trudy off ledges. This was a ledge. "Don't get your feathers in a ruffle. Nobody's going to care about the chairs when they see how pretty it looks out there. And when Jenna walks out, looking lovely in her wedding dress, that's all they'll see."

Trudy looked stricken. "*I care.* And Jenna too."

Gert couldn't care less. Her café had an assortment of chairs and tables that she'd thrown in there years ago when she opened the little place. She hadn't had the extra money to buy matching chairs. Instead, she'd shopped junk stores and bought every cheap-priced chair she could find. And the booths had been made out of simple lumber. She was not fancy. And her style had worked just fine all these years. She was relieved when Sally Ann came around the corner. "There's Sally Ann. Ask her. You know she won't care about the color of the chairs. Her bed-and-breakfast is full of furniture from her junk shop and people love to come spend the weekend there."

"But this is a wedding!" Trudy cried one more time.

"What in the world has you turning red as the roses in my niece's wedding bouquet?" Sally Ann cocked her bleach-blonde head to the side, giving Trudy a hard study. "You're not sick, are you?"

Trudy threw up her hands. "Yes, I am sick. I'm sick about the brown chairs. My Shane and your Jenna should have the wedding they wanted and these brown chairs are awful."

Sally Ann threw her head back and howled with laughter. "I love you dearly, Trudy-girl, but you are too high-strung. Gert, didn't you tell her the chairs don't matter?"

"Well, of course I did. Over and over. But she's got herself all lathered up and I'm figuring we're going to have to stick her under a cold shower to cool her down."

"You two just don't understand—"

"We do too." Sally Ann put her arm around Trudy's shoulders and gave her a squeeze. "You want the best for your nephews and since you're representing their sweet, deceased mama, you feel the pressure of that and you want them all to have perfect weddings."

Trudy teared up. "Yes. It's an honor but a lot of pressure. And the chairs just got me."

"And Cooper and Beth's wedding was certainly beautiful and they are as happy as can be. And even if something had gone wrong, they'd still be just as happy. Shane and Jenna will be too, and the chairs do not matter a lick. Okay? Repeat my words. The chairs don't matter a lick."

Gert put her arm around Trudy's waist and gave

her a supportive hug and a smile. "You can do it."

Trudy took a deep breath and her color eased up. "The chairs don't matter a lick."

"There you go." Sally Ann wrapped an arm around her from the other side.

"What would I do without you two?" Trudy asked.

Gert hitched a brow at her. "Probably be a pure mess with all that lather you work up, my high-strung friend."

"She's excitable," Sally Ann quipped.

"I am. It's true. Thank you, girls. I guess we better get busy."

Gert was relieved when Trudy smiled. And then laughed.

They had been through a lot together and knew each one had the other's back. They'd all been friends for a long time. After Trudy's sister-in-law died giving birth to Lana, the baby of the family, Trudy had stepped in to help raise all these Presley men and sweet Lana. Her brother, Marcus, had needed the help because he had to run the ranch too. But Trudy could get herself into dithers sometimes over non-important details because she felt the pressure to fill in the hole their mother had left. She had done a good job; all the kids loved her and had grown into good men and Lana into a good woman. And they couldn't care less about chairs.

Sally Ann gave her friend a last squeeze and let her go as she focused on Gert. "So, now that the meltdown is averted and there's a smile on Trudy's face, tell us if that cute Libby is coming to the wedding?"

"She wasn't going to come. So, I had to go to plan number two and told her that I really needed her to help me serve. I know we wanted her here as a guest but she just wasn't taking the bait. So, relax—she will be here. We just might have to grab dishes out of her hands every time Vance comes around. And I have a feeling after the way your Vance was looking at her yesterday that he's going to ask her to dance, even if he has to dodge wedding cake splatters on his boots."

Trudy clasped her hands together and smiled. "He does seem smitten with her. And the sweet girl is certainly smitten with him."

"She is at that," Gert said. "But she's so shy and secretive, I don't know if she'll give him the time of day."

Sally Ann's eyes twinkled. "If a Presley wants a lady to pay attention to him, he just has to turn on the charm, and that cutie-patootie Vance just has to make those pretty eyes of his twinkle. She'll come around."

It was true, Gert hoped. "There's just something about Libby that makes me want every good thing in the world for her. I don't even know where she came from or what caused her to hitchhike here but maybe Vance can talk her into a dance tonight and a little fun. Who knows what might come of it."

"Agreed," Sally Ann declared.

"Yes, I agree too," Trudy said. "I just hope she's not here because she's in some kind of trouble."

"We've already discussed this," Sally Ann said. "If she is, we'll help her."

Gert nodded. She just really hoped Libby wasn't in some kind of deep trouble. But the sheriff didn't think so; at least, when she'd asked him, he had told her he didn't think she was. That was good. She hoped he was right.

"Well, now that we have Trudy calmed down, I'm going to go check out the food for the reception. I'm expecting my help, including Libby, to get here soon. I want everything ready so it will run smoothly as soon as the preacher pronounces these two as man and wife."

"Thank you, Gert. You and Sally Ann are the best girlfriends a gal could have. Thanks for understanding too."

"Hey, any time. You'd do the same for me."

"True, I would. Not that you ever need it, though."

Sally Ann grinned. "Yep, our Gert's tough as nails, even being a short little squirt."

They all laughed. Gert waved and headed off toward the food tent. She was short but had always prided herself in being steady and strong. But like anyone, she had her moments; everyone did. It was good to have friends like Sally Ann and Trudy.

They did like to meddle a bit, though, but the way she viewed it, sometimes folks needed a bit of meddling in order for the best for them to come through. The thing was, Vance Presley seemed intrigued enough with Libby that she wasn't so sure they were going to need to do much meddling. Other than making sure Libby arrived at the wedding, and that was already taken care of. Now to just sit back and watch nature take its course.

Libby tugged at the dress that had been in the grouping that Sally Ann had given her from several of the younger ladies in town. Libby hadn't wanted to accept the clothes, but Miss Sally Ann had been about as kind and straightforward as could be when she'd insisted. She'd said everyone had noticed she didn't have anything but the clothes on her back and they wanted to pitch in and help her feel welcome and to look at the clothes as housewarming gifts. That had made Libby smile considering she was really only staying temporarily in the apartment above the café. But she could really use the clothes and had agreed finally. But this was the first time she'd worn any of the dresses and it felt strange because she'd been wearing only jeans and blouses for months now.

Feeling out of place here, she glanced around from where she was partly hidden by a large green flowering bush in a pot that had been placed on either side of the main entrance into the canopy. She'd arrived a little late, having waited to ride to the wedding with Rosemary, the caterer delivering the meal, instead of with Gert, who had come out early to be with Trudy. This was as it should be because they were very close, but Libby would have felt out of place. She also was trying to avoid being around Vance Presley.

Leaning forward for a better view of the wedding, she watched as Jenna and Shane held hands and gazed into each other's eyes. A pang of her own wedding day happiness ached in her heart. The preacher looked from one to the other. She was so happy for them.

Unwanted, her gaze strayed to Vance. He stood tall and straight and her aching heart slammed against her chest when, after a second, his gaze found hers. It was as if he felt her looking at him. She pulled back behind the bush, wishing she hadn't come. Wishing she hadn't agreed to help oversee the food.

Miss Gert had tried to get her to come over to the area in the pretty pasture where the wedding was taking place and sit with her, but Libby just couldn't let herself do that.

She couldn't help envy the Presleys and their close-knit relationship. Coming from a background that had almost no family ties, it was something she longed for.

The preacher pronounced them husband and wife and the music swelled as Shane took Jenna into his arms and kissed her tenderly. Long and slow, it was just about the most romantic thing she'd ever seen. Then he held her close for a moment before letting her go, cherishing her.

She'd had that and lost it. And just as she'd feared, the wedding caused her heart to ache for what she'd lost.

Her throat swelled as they faced the crowd and tears burned in her eyes. She looked away, her gaze automatically flickering to Vance.

He was watching her.

She gasped and though the need to draw back out

of sight was great, she couldn't move. She barely knew the cowboy and yet, every ounce of her soul told her he could mean the world to her if she could let him in. That very idea frightened her.

She didn't want anyone to ever mean the world to her again.

Ever.

Forcing her legs to move, she stepped behind the bush, praying her thundering heart and weak knees would straighten up.

CHAPTER THREE

Libby hurried toward the reception tent, brushing away tears. She hoped she didn't look as if she'd been crying. She took a steadying breath before entering the tent and fought to find the poker face that had been her go-to expression since burying Mark, until lately, when it had suddenly started to falter.

Rosemary, a plump woman with naturally rose-tinted cheeks, smiled at her from where she was checking the dishes. She'd sent Libby to see how the ceremony was going.

"Are they Mr. and Mrs. Presley yet?" She beamed

expectantly.

"Just now," she managed, glad she had overcome the lump in her throat and the tears.

"Good. Good. Things are ready here. Would you be a dear and come back here behind the table with me? As soon as they start forming lines, you can remove all the lids and set them on that nice table over there. I've already checked the readiness of all the dishes, so we are all set. All but me preparing the punch at just the right moment, so that's what I'll be taking care of over by the cake."

"I'd be happy to do whatever you need me to do." *Happy to disappear if possible*. But at least the table put a barrier between her and everyone. She had been struggling to keep distance between her and all these wonderful people from the moment she'd arrived in town. But it was getting harder to do with each day she remained here. And that was the problem: the closer she got to them, the more she could be hurt.

She just couldn't take any more hurt. As a child, she'd lived through tragedy when she lost her parents in a boating accident. She'd withdrawn but learned to be independent and fairly happy, though she'd grown up at a girls' ranch in west Texas. It had been a foster home to a good number of teenage girls. And though it was a blessing in her life, she'd never grown close to anyone. Until Mark had arrived at the nearby boys' ranch. They'd met at a combined ranch function and he'd slowly won her trust and her heart. At eighteen, as soon as the foster system cut them loose, they'd married.

They'd struggled but they'd been happy. So happy. They might not have had anyone else but they had each other.

For five years. Long enough to start saving a little for a house and planning for a future.

And then everything had fallen apart. Everything had changed—

Stop thinking about it.

She was thankful in the next moment when Miss Gert came hustling into the tent. She was all grins as she caught sight of Libby.

"That was about the sweetest wedding I've seen. Thank you for helping Rosemary but you both should have come to see the actual wedding. I saved two seats near the back."

Rosemary hustled from the preparation area behind a curtain, carrying a container full of peach-colored punch. "Now you know I'm not one to sit down in crowds for long."

"I know and you're a doll for what you do. But, Libby, you could have come."

"I told her as much," Rosemary said.

Libby gave a weak smile. "I feel better here too." *If Rosemary could get away with it, maybe she could too.*

Gert clucked her tongue and shook her head. "Well, fine. But, let's get the covers off this food and herd everyone in here, *then* you can be free to mingle a bit." She grinned impishly.

Libby fought not to adore the small woman with the larger-than-life heart. In the short time she'd been here, Gert had been the grandmother she'd never had. The mother she'd never had. It would be hard to let her go.

But she would. "Miss Gert, I didn't come to

mingle. I'm just fine standing back here making sure the serving trays are full."

Her expression drooped. "Did you think I was going to have you come out here and serve all evening and not expect you to have a little fun? Nope, not happening. I'm expecting you to dance the night away, young lady."

"But I really can't dance." Mark hadn't danced either and that had been fine with her. He'd loved other things, like hiking, and they'd both enjoyed riding horses, which was something both the girls' ranch and the boys' ranch had taught them. After leaving, they hadn't had the opportunity to ride any more. She quickly added, "I don't like to dance."

"Hogwash. All young ladies like to dance, if the right cowboy asks them to. And I have high hopes for you this evening. Besides, once we take the lids off this BBQ, there really isn't much left to do. That's what the beauty of a laid-back reception is—everyone just makes themselves at home."

Libby was about to say something when the smiling wedding party headed into the tent. She didn't waste time getting behind the tables and hurried to remove the lids and place them on the table behind her. Thankfully she wouldn't be carrying dishes this evening. With the tension she was dealing with, her and plates…and Vance…could mean total disaster.

Her skin tingled with goose bumps. Lifting her eyes from the pan of barbequed brisket she was uncovering, she surveyed the tent.

She found Vance watching her.

A longing slammed into her so overwhelmingly that it nearly cut her legs out from under her. He nodded at her from across the room, his eyes seeming to heat her skin and caress her at the same time. She stiffened at the thought but more because the feelings were so intense.

To her relief, as if sensing he made her nervous, he touched the lip of his hat then moved away to talk with his dad and the pretty lady whose arm was linked with his. She'd seen them in the café together a few times and Gert had mentioned that she was sure glad he was finally dating Karla after all these years since his wife died. She empathized with him deeply, knowing the heartache he must have felt after losing his wife in childbirth. It surely had to be fierce, with a house full of boys waiting on him to bring their mom and baby sister home. She'd had to mourn only for her loss and couldn't imagine the depth of what he must have felt mourning for himself and them too.

She was grateful when Bella Anderson, who was married to Vance's cousin Carson, came to stand beside her. It helped reel in her thoughts. Bella's specialty was putting on events so, despite Miss Gert being in charge of the food, Bella was the main boss of the wedding event.

"I just wanted to come thank you for helping out." Bella smiled brightly.

She really liked Bella. She liked all the women she'd met who were associated with the Presley brothers. They were a lucky bunch of women: Bella, Beth, Jenna and she included Lori Jensen in that group, too, because she was married to their friend Trip, a very nice guy when he came into the café. She noticed because there were a few rowdy cowboys in the area but Miss Gert didn't put up with any shenanigans, as she called bad behavior. And they knew if they wanted to eat, they had to behave. That didn't mean Libby hadn't felt their eyes follow her around. Why she was suddenly thinking of Grady Black, she wasn't sure. He wasn't here—as far as she'd seen, anyway—and that was good.

She smiled at Bella. "I'm happy to help out. You've all been so good to me since I came to town. I like giving back. I told Miss Gert I didn't want to get paid. This is my wedding gift to Shane and Jenna."

"Nonsense. Of course we're paying you for your time here. If you want to get them a gift, then you're free to do it with a little of the money we pay you but you will be getting a check."

"Really, I don't want it."

"You're getting it and that's final. Now, I'm hoping you take time to enjoy yourself too. That means when the dinner is over you'll come to the dance. Better yet, come join the guests now. These dishes are made for everyone to serve themselves."

"But I need to keep an eye on things." She knew she sounded almost desperate.

"That's fine. But when the music starts, please join in on the dancing. I'm sure there are plenty of single cowboys out there who will be asking."

"But—"

"Please—you are a part of our community and you serve us when we come to the diner. I'd like you to have at least part of the night off for socializing. You deserve it. And Jenna and Shane have specifically asked me to pass that on to you in case they don't get to do it themselves."

How could she refuse the bride and groom? "Okay, I will after everyone has their food."

Bella smiled. "Wonderful. Now, I better go make sure my daughter isn't playing hide-and-seek under the tables. These long tablecloths and glassware make that a very dangerous game."

"I just saw her with Cooper a few minutes ago. They both wore mischievous expressions, so I'm not sure if that's a help or not."

Bella chuckled. "Knowing Cooper, they have something planned. They may be putting sardines in the bride and groom's truck or some other wedding prank."

Despite the turmoil she'd been feeling moments ago, this made Libby both laugh and cringe.

Just then, Shane and Jenna entered the tent, with the photographer trailing close. The cowboy preacher was with them also and as soon as the crowd saw them, everyone turned their way.

"Ladies and gentlemen," the preacher said in a deep, resounding voice. "May I present to you, Mr. and Mrs. Shane Presley."

Boisterous clapping and loud whistles ensued.

As soon as the clapping began to calm, Gert waved toward the buffet. "And with that, you two lead the way and let's get this dinner started. Y'all have a wedding dance to get to."

That brought on more cheers and some teasing.

"Are you two going to give us a *Dancing with the Stars* exhibition dance?" Cooper called through cupped hands.

"Maybe a ballroom two-step," Brice added as laughter broke out.

Shane shot them a good-natured grin. "You just

have to wait and see. Y'all know I got all the moves in the family."

"Not unless you borrowed Vance's body for the event," Drake called.

"Hey, I'm not bad either," Cooper interjected.

"Maybe we need a brother against brother dance-off at some point tonight," Trip Jensen called out.

Cooper's hand went up. "I'm all in if you fellas think you can handle it."

Libby was in awe of them and their teasing. She also realized that Vance was just leaning casually against a pole with his arms crossed, smiling quietly and watching his brothers.

She liked his quiet, easy attitude and for some reason, she had a feeling that Drake hadn't been kidding about Vance being the best dancer.

"I'll referee when the time comes," Marcus said. "But right now, let's eat."

Jenna picked up a plate, smiling at the fun. As Shane moved closer to her and took a plate, she leaned her head against his chest briefly in a show of love.

Libby looked away, not wanting to intrude. She

stirred the potatoes that didn't need stirring.

When Jenna reached her, the pretty bride leaned across the potatoes and gently grasped Libby's arm. "Thank you so much. You, Gert, and Rosemary are doing an amazing job."

Shane agreed. "Yes, and we really appreciate each of you."

A warm satisfaction filled her. "I'm happy to help. Congratulations to both of you." She prayed really hard that they lived a very long, happy life together.

Jenna beamed at Shane. "We're so happy. Thank you."

After they'd moved on, the line moved quickly and Libby stayed busy refilling the serving dishes with the extras heating behind the curtain. Rosemary, finished with the punch, helped, while Gert moved about the room, chatting and refilling beverages.

"Penny for your thoughts," a warm, deep voice said from behind her as the line had finished and people were returning for seconds.

Her pulse skittered, as she recognized Vance's

voice close to her ear. She turned to find him smiling and standing a foot from her.

He winked. "I decided since you weren't holding any plates or platters that now was a good time to approach you."

She blushed and tried to form words but for a moment, her brain was scrambled. His nearness and the uncanny resemblance to Mark had her speechless.

"You're really shy, aren't you?" He smiled that crooked, kind smile that reached his teasing, green eyes.

She wasn't as quiet as she seemed to everyone in Ransom Creek. A combination of several factors had her subdued since arriving in the small town. Part of which was the overwhelming attraction to Vance and her need not to be. It was something she could not wrap her mind around nor accept. She wasn't ready to move on but she knew soon she would have to if this continued. She couldn't fathom opening herself up to the possibility of getting close to anyone. Especially someone who reminded her so much of her late husband. Her best friend. The love of her life.

"I'm quiet," she said, her thoughts reeling. "And a bit clumsy sometimes," she added and took a step back from Vance.

His smile widened, making her knees weaken. "I've figured that out. I just haven't figured out why you're just clumsy around me."

She wasn't sure whether he was teasing her or whether he really didn't know why she got that way when he walked into a room. She certainly wasn't going to tell him. She hitched one shoulder and gave a smile that probably looked more like the grimace it felt like.

The man was a lethal weapon.

Not giving up, he cocked his head to the side. "I think the whole matter requires some investigation into what the problem might be. So that's why I'm hoping you'll save a dance or two for me after dinner." He held his hand up for her to halt when she started to interrupt him. "No need to answer, since I know you're quiet. Just think about it and be ready. I've got to go sit with the wedding party at the front table but when the dancing starts, I'll be back."

And then, with a tip of his hat, he strode away and left her with a smile on her lips.

The man was cute. Too cute. And she was not going to dance with him. No matter how much she realized she wanted to.

It wouldn't be smart.

Not smart at all.

CHAPTER FOUR

"You two were getting cozy over there, with that long conversation," Brice said as Vance took his seat next to him at the wedding party table. "And I didn't hear the sound of plates hitting the ground either, so you're making progress."

"I waited until she wasn't carrying plates and snuck up on her."

"Smart thinking. From here, she looked like she actually talked a little too."

"Yeah, the operative word being *little*. She's just quiet. But I get the feeling there's more to it than that.

She promised me a dance though," she hadn't actually said yes but he was thinking positive. "And I'm thinking I might get a date before the evening is over if I play my cards right. I'm feeling pretty lucky tonight."

"Hey, you should. She hasn't given any of the cowboys who've gone into the diner a second look since she got into town. And y'all do have that sexy plate dropping thing going on."

Vance chuckled. "That's because I'm special and don't you forget it, brother."

"Ha! I'd say dropped on your head by a bronc a few too many times. But I'll agree that you don't give up. Persistent and determined. That's what you are."

He grinned. "That I agree with. And we'll see who's special when I beat y'all on the dance floor challenge later."

Brice frowned. "We're not really doing that."

"I think we are. If Cooper and Drake have their way."

"I'm not doing that. No way. You know good and well you got all the right feet and I got the wrong feet."

Vance grimaced. If Brice could tease him about

Libby dropping dishes, then he could take some of his own medicine because it was true. Brice had two left feet when it came to dancing. His rhythm was off and needed help. "Hey, all you have to do is find a dance teacher somewhere and get some lessons, cowboy."

"I'm not taking lessons. And I'm not doing a dance challenge."

Lana was sitting across from them and had been in deep conversation with Cam. Now, she leaned toward them. "If you don't want to, you don't have to. Cam could take your place."

"What?" Cam asked, realizing she'd just spoken for him. "Darlin', I only dance with you these days and doing a line dance with your brothers does not count."

"Well, if you put it that way, I guess you're off the hook." She kissed Cam's cheek and he and Brice glanced at each other.

"It sure has gotten mushy around here lately," Brice said.

Lana leaned her head on Cam's shoulder. "One day, big brother, you'll understand."

Vance liked the look of love in his baby sister's

eyes. She was happy. Fed up with her meddling brothers, she'd run as far away from them as she could get, taking a teaching job in Windswept Bay, a picturesque island off the coast of St. Petersburg, Florida where Cam Sinclair's family owned a beach resort and she'd met him. As fate would have it, they'd been blessed to learn that Cam had just been visiting there and really owned a ranch a few short hours from them here in Texas.

Cam kissed the top of her head. "Are you feeling okay?" he heard Cam murmur for her ears only.

Vance heard the question then realized that Lana looked pale and hadn't eaten hardly anything on her plate. He hadn't either but he was about to. She, on the other hand, looked as if eating was the last thing she'd be doing.

Drake stood up to give the best man speech. It was still hard for Vance to realize that his brothers were systematically falling in love and getting married. It was as though when their friends Trip and Lori had finally realized they loved each other and they'd tied the knot, the dominos started to fall. First, Cousin Carson falling for Bella and then Cooper and Beth, and now Shane and Jenna. Seriously, it was more like a rampaging fire burning its way through them, one at a time. But it really all started with Lana and Cam. He glanced at Brice then back at Drake and wondered who would be next.

Logically, it would be Drake; he was the oldest and Vance figured his oldest brother would be looking to settle down any day. But him—he wasn't ready. He had a championship to win and needed to keep his focus.

As Drake started speaking, Vance found Libby in the crowd. She'd sat with Miss. Gert and looked as if she were enjoying herself. Her gaze met his and he winked. Couldn't help himself. When she looked at him, he felt this deep need to make her smile and to reassure her that things were okay.

She surprised him when she gave him a small smile before looking down at her plate.

Drake started talking and he pulled his gaze away

from her to give Drake his attention.

"What can I say about my brother Shane? First, Cooper," Drake was saying, "found a wife while rescuing a baby goat wearing a red dress. Shane couldn't be outdone and found himself a wife by rescuing her off the side of the road on a freezing night." The statements brought instant laughter and clapping from the crowd, who all knew it was true.

Vance picked his glass up and took a drink, thinking about later when he planned to sweep the quiet Libby into his arms and dance her around the dance floor. The thought was as consuming as that key moment when he lowered himself into the rodeo chute and the saddle of a champion class bronc. He was hyper focused on the bronc in that moment.

And right now, thinking about Libby in his arms had his full attention.

Even overshadowing his celebrating Shane and Jenna's wedding.

Right after the dinner was over, Miss Gert banned her

from cleanup and told her to mingle and to get ready to dance. So here she stood, beside a tall table with a flickering Mason jar candle in its center and pretty greenery as the centerpiece. It was an amazing night with the big Texas sky, black as coal, and thousands of stars clearly visible, hanging like a canopy over the dance area. The large wooden dance floor had been set up in the backyard area of the big ranch house. More battery powered candles flickered inside Mason jars hung from the cedar fence that surrounded the yard. Beautiful swags of intertwined greenery, lace, and fairy lights cascaded over the rough wood fence. And fairy lights strung above the dance floor completed the look. It was very romantic and lovely.

The nervous energy her insides were spinning could have powered the abundance of fairy lights. Purposefully, she had chosen the table in the darkest shadows of the lawn and watched as Shane and Jenna danced together to one of her favorite older but great waltzes, "When I Said I Do," by Clint Black and his wife Lisa Hartman Black. They danced together gracefully to the beautiful song. Memories of the quick civil ceremony that she and Mark had shared came to mind. They'd been so young and so in love that standing there, trembling with happiness before the judge, had been romantic enough. But this, this was a fairy-tale Western wedding and she was enjoying watching Shane and Jenna's happiness.

Then the wedding party took their turn on the dance floor and obviously the paired-off groomsmen and bridesmaids had prepared their dances, along with Jenna and Shane. The tune was a fast country song and completely let them let loose. And all the Presley brothers who were present did just that. She had never seen so much action on a dance floor. The bridesmaids were spun, dipped, lifted, and twirled as the brothers' boots worked double time on fancy footwork. She found herself smiling. Clapping started almost as soon as the dance began and she felt as if she were watching a dance-off contest. Amid all of it, there was Vance, long and lean and as graceful and laid-back as it got. The cowboy stood out as he led his bridesmaid through a jitterbug that was smokin' hot, it was so fast. His partner—someone she didn't know, and probably one of Jenna's friends from Seattle, where she'd worked before—also knew her way around a dance floor. Vance held his hand above her head, and he and she both spun around the dance floor faster than the teacups at a theme park.

Wow. Just wow. That was all Libby's mind could express as she watched them end the dance on a bang when Vance suddenly dropped to the dance floor in a split and then somehow popped back to standing in almost the same move.

How was that even possible?

The moment he was standing, he yanked his shirttail from his waistband, whispered something in the ear of his partner then disappeared down a side path toward the house.

The thrill of the dance was replaced by a letdown feeling as she watched the vacant shadows where he'd disappeared.

Was he gone for the evening? What did it matter? She wasn't going to dance with him anyway. Especially after seeing that. The man could win dance competitions, for crying out loud.

Still, the thought of being held in his arms as they gently swayed to soft music filled her with a sudden longing and sent butterflies into flight inside her.

She toyed with a napkin and thought about quietly slipping away and going home but she didn't have a car. She wondered how long it would be before Vance returned, if he returned. *And if he did, when would he ask her to dance?*

What did it matter anyway? She decided while she sat through all the sweet speeches for Shane and Jenna that one dance would be okay. *One dance and that was it.* He had been very kind to her and it was nice of him to ask. But now, after seeing him dance, she would feel gawky and silly dancing with him.

Still, there was that part of her that longed to see whether Vance Presley was as wonderful as he seemed.

"Hi, Libby." Lana Sinclair stood beside her. "Thanks so much for helping out tonight."

Libby had met Lana at the diner a couple of times when she'd come to visit and help with the wedding plans. She resembled her brothers very much but instead of handsome, she was beautiful, with her dark hair and sparkling eyes. "I'm glad I could. And it was so nice."

"Yes, it was. And now the dancing. I always get a kick out of watching my brothers tear up a dance floor. All of them—except Brice, who is a little less skilled—can hold their own out there. Especially Vance. Brice always teases him that he got both of their dance talent." She chuckled. "After watching him do that calf roping step, as I like to call it, I might agree with poor Brice."

"Calf roping step? You mean that split that he did? I can't wrap my mind around what I saw, it was so unusual. I'd never get down there and if I did, I certainly would not be able to get up, much less pop up like he did."

Lana chuckled. "Calf ropers need to be limber for their competition. Hopping off a horse practically running at full speed and then grabbing a calf takes a knee in the dirt and a wide stance to get the calf grabbed and flipped and tied in record winning time. Being limber keeps them healthy. Before Vance concentrated on saddle bronc riding as his competition to compete for the NFR, he was really good at calf roping. He's naturally limber. Like a cat."

"Oh, I see. He was amazing. And intimidating. Goodness, if you stink at dancing, it would show even more if you were dancing with him."

"No, don't say that. He's a very, very good teacher. I'm thrilled you're here for this dance and"— her eyes flickered past Libby, and then came back to her, twinkling—"when he asks you to dance, I hope you say yes."

"I do too." Vance leaned over her shoulder and smiled as he slid in beside her at the table.

"Great to talk to you. I need to find a chair and sit down for a little while. It's been a long day."

"Good talking to you too," Libby said.

Before Lana could get away, Vance slipped his arm over his sister's shoulders and kissed her on the cheek. "Not so fast, sis. Are you feeling okay? You looked pale at dinner."

"I'm just tired. I didn't sleep well last night. Don't worry about me, I'm fine. Have fun, you two."

Libby watched the care between the two as Lana

planted a kiss on his five o'clock shadowed jaw. "Love you."

"Ditto, kiddo."

A sharp pang of jealousy hit Libby as she watched them. *Family—this was as good as it got.*

He watched Lana walk away then smiled at Libby. "You are looking stunning tonight."

Libby couldn't help smiling, even though she knew her light-brown hair and pixie face were far from stunning. "I think those splits you did addled your brain." The words were out before she could stop them.

He laughed. "I can assure you it did not. You are stunning. That blue dress makes your blue eyes look deep enough to swim in."

"Oh," slipped out. It was all she could say.

"Speaking of dances, I came to claim my dance before a rush of cowboys come over here and try to hog you all night."

Heat leaped in her chest and took off down the racetrack at lightning speed. She couldn't breathe as a new song started. It was a soft, slow country song meant for holding someone close.

"May I have this dance?"

His eyes drilled into hers with a pull she couldn't resist. She nodded. Her heart hammered as his smile widened and he took her hand and stepped back, drawing her with him onto the dance floor. His hand was warm and firm, not too tight but just right as he held hers. There was a protective feeling in the way he held her hand and then he tugged her gently into his arms and ever so barely against him. She knew he could probably feel the pounding of her heart even though she wasn't pressed intimately against him. She looked at him.

He smiled. "I've been waiting all night for this moment. And I was afraid you might not stick around for the dance." His expression turned serious. "I'm glad you did."

She had been looking up at him and couldn't believe she was here in his arms, so close to him that if she leaned her head in just slightly, she could feel the soft scrape of his five o'clock shadow. *Or, if she lifted on her toes, she might be able to kiss his perfect lips.*

What was she thinking? "Me too," she croaked.

He grinned. "You sure are pretty when you blush." And then he spun her away from him and back.

She laughed in startled surprise when she landed with a hard thump against his chest.

He chuckled, and hugged her close. "Sorry, my bad," he murmured, gazing into her eyes. Mesmerizing her. And then he danced them in an easy sweep around the dance floor.

In a world that suddenly seemed to be made up of only them.

"You have me more and more curious about you with every moment I'm with you," he said. The warmth of his breath caressed her ear as he leaned in slightly for her to hear him as they were closer to the band now. "Do you like to mountain climb?"

The serious question caught her unexpectedly. "Um, no, I'm scared of heights. I mean, I hike but not too high."

"Good. Not that you're scared of heights but that you don't like to rock climb because I don't either."

"Then why did you ask me?" She laughed.

His grin was infectious as he tilted his head and leaned his forehead against hers. "To get a reaction from you. And I need to know if the girl I'm trying hard to get to know is more adventurous than me. I have to say, I'm relieved you don't like mountain climbing. That's about the most intimidating thing I can think of."

She liked the way they were touching. Liked the way he was teasing her. She just liked everything about him. "You don't have to be intimidated about anything about me. I'm not climbing a mountain, jumping out of an airplane, or riding a bucking bronco in a rodeo like you do."

He pulled back and gaped at her. "Do you realize you just said more words to me in that statement than you've said in all the other meetings put together?"

"I speak. I just seem to have a problem when you're around," she admitted, honestly. "You know, with dropping the plates and all."

The song ended but he held her in place. "New song's coming." And it did and he started them dancing again. "Libby, I'm hoping that after tonight, you won't be dropping plates anymore. I thought if we got to know each other, you'd realize I'm not a bad person."

Her feet stumbled. "It had nothing to do with me thinking you were a bad person. It was that I find you—" She clammed up.

"You find me…what?"

She stared up at him. She found him irresistible, undeniably attractive, and hard to look away from. But she could not tell him that.

After a moment, his lips twitched. He spun her easily around with him, causing her to feel a little like Cinderella finding her prince.

He rested his jaw against her ear. "I'll tell you how I feel. I find you irresistible."

She had no words. None.

And he didn't say more as they danced quietly for a few stanzas of the Lady Antebellum song. When it came to an end, far sooner than she was ready for, he didn't let go of her hand as they walked off the dance floor. "Would you go out with me?"

Her world spun with the way he was looking at her, as if he wasn't just saying idle compliments. She shook her head, her senses seeping back in. "You don't want to go out with me."

His brows dipped. "I do. Why would you say I wouldn't?"

Uncomfortable emotions washed over her. "I'm not…it just wouldn't work."

"You know, if you don't want to go out with me, you can say so."

He thought she didn't like him. The idea threw her completely off. "No, I…it's just that you're really outgoing and I'm not. And my life is complicated right now."

His beautiful eyes narrowed. "I'm outgoing enough for both of us, so no worries about that. I could talk the bricks off the side of a house if I needed to. But, I'm also a good listener if you need to talk. I mean, complications can seem less complicated if you talk them out."

They stared at each other and she longed to

confide in him. *Which was absurd. She wasn't going to spill her guts to this guy.* She couldn't stand the thought of watching that sweet twinkle of flirtation flickered out. "Thank you for the dance. It was…lovely. But I can't go out with you." There, she had spoken the words, despite wishing she could go out with him and actually get to know him.

The man made her feel good simply by looking at her. *How was that possible?*

"You're breaking my heart," he teased.

"I'm sure that's not true."

He smiled. "If you can't go out with me, how about dancing with me again?" He hitched his brow and dipped his chin as he took her hand and tugged her back toward the dance floor.

She could not resist his playful antics. *What could it really hurt?*

His arms were around her, holding her carefully as they moved to the slow music. They danced for a long time, not saying anything, just moving with the beat in a slow country two-step. She felt as if she'd stepped into a country fairy tale...she was enjoying herself too much. Reality suddenly intruded, causing her pulse to quicken. She stopped dancing as her thoughts went to Mark. *What was she doing?*

"I can't," she gasped as she looked up at Vance. "I'm sorry. What was I thinking?" She pulled away and hurried toward the parking lot. Tears blinded her as she ran.

What, oh what, had she been thinking?

CHAPTER FIVE

Vance watched Libby race blindly from the dance floor. The expression of utter despair that had been on her face when she'd looked up at him had broken his heart and frozen him to the spot when she'd spun and raced away from him. He'd finally reacted and hurried after her. *What was going on?*

"Vance, what's wrong with Libby?" Drake asked as he was passing him.

"I'm not sure. I've got to catch her. Talk later," he said, keeping after her.

"Call me if I can help," Drake offered.

Vance jogged to catch Libby. "Wait, Libby. Please."

When she paused, he gently took her arm. Her shoulders were shaking and he knew she was crying before he turned her around. He wasn't prepared for the way seeing tears streaming down her face broke his heart into a million pieces. He crumbled on the inside.

"Aw, Libby, what's the matter, sugar?" His arms wrapped around her automatically, the need so overwhelming he couldn't have stopped himself if he'd wanted to. She collapsed against his chest and wept. *Wept as if her heart were breaking.*

"Let it out," he said, his throat clogging with emotions. He cupped her soft hair with his hand and caressed it, wanting to comfort her in any way he could. Something was going on that only she knew but he could tell it wasn't good. *But what had he done to bring this on?* "It's going to be all right, whatever it is that you're dealing with. Just let it out." He tried, but felt incapable of expressing the right words to such deep pain.

All he knew he could do was stand firm and hold

her.

He hoped the soft music from the wedding that drifted to them as the band started up again would soothe her. But she'd become upset while dancing, so he wasn't sure whether the sound was good or bad. *Was it the dance or was it him?* The thought that he could have had a part in causing her tears cut him to the core.

"I'm sorry," she whispered, the sound muffled against his crisp white button-down.

"Not a problem. You cry all you want if it helps."

"Thank you," she said, her voice still so soft he had to lean in closer to hear her.

"No need to thank me. I'm just hoping I'm not the reason you're crying."

"You aren't. Well, not directly." She sniffed and then raised her gaze to meet his.

He had a knee-jerk reaction to seeing her big blue eyes misted with tears. He had never reacted to a woman like he was responding to Libby Smith.

The urge to kiss her temple slammed into him...in comfort. But there was a deep longing to kiss her lips and at the moment it felt wrong. But it was there, strong and growing, but would have to wait until she wasn't in distress. What she'd just said finally reached past his distracting thoughts. "Wait, what do you mean not directly?"

Her gaze shifted away from him. "You remind me of someone. And that's both a good thing and a bad thing at the same time, that's all." She looked back at him almost with apology.

His heart sank. "This person means a lot to you?"

She took a long breath, as if steadying her nerves and in the end, just gave a quick nod.

He'd known it before she confirmed it for him. She must have gone through a hard breakup. Or she and this guy were having a big fight and she was sad about it. If that was it, she was definitely in love with the guy. He wasn't sure what to feel about that. Disappointed that she was hurting this much over someone else? And the fact that that pretty much wiped his chances away. They were still staring at each other, so close.

He found his voice again. "Can I help in any way?

You obviously care about him."

Her lips lifted and she nodded. "I need to go. Miss Gert only needed me for the meal. I'm sorry." She stepped out of his embrace and for a moment looked uncertain, as if she wanted to return to his arms.

Which might have just been wishful thinking on his part. "Are you sure you are okay to drive? I can drive you."

"I'm fine. But thank you for watching out for me."

"My pleasure. Anytime." He watched her walking away from him and felt as if his world had just narrowed to a single vision set on her.

And she was walking away.

"I mean it, Libby. Anytime, or *anything* you need, just ask and I'll help."

She turned and gave a weak smile, a sad smile that cut him even deeper, and then she walked away and he could only watch helplessly.

And then it hit him. "Libby," he called, jogging to where she'd stopped and hung her head. "Did you get a car?"

She let out an exasperated sigh. "No. I was so

upset I forgot I don't have a ride. I came with one of the other ladies helping with the catering and I was going to ride back to town with Miss Gert." Her expression was bleak.

It might have been bad on his part but his spirits lifted. "I'll give you a ride and I'll text Gert and let her know you're with me."

His head was spinning, realizing that she'd been so upset she'd forgotten she didn't have a car. *What had happened to her?* One thing was certain—he was determined to find out.

What are you doing? What are you doing? What are you doing?

Her voice of reason screeched over and over as Libby rode with Vance in the close quarters of his truck and the dark night made a cocoon around them. Fighting the darkness in her soul, she tried desperately to remain calm and not let herself fall apart.

Her thoughts swirled and she fought for footing. So not expecting to be here in this moment when she'd gone on the run nearly two months ago.

And now, here she was in his truck after having spent the evening dancing with the man. She couldn't do this and she knew it. She'd leave first thing in the morning. She had to. Her heart was in an uncertain place and she wasn't sure what to do.

Run was the only thing she could do.

"Libby, I'm going to be frank with you." Vance's quiet voice broke the silence. "Something is wrong and I have a terrible feeling you need to talk about it. I can't get it off my mind that you are in trouble."

So much trouble. She took a deep breath, trying to calm her nerves, trying to calm the turmoil tearing her up inside. Maybe it was the darkness, giving her some semblance of shelter, or the gentle timbre of Vance's voice. Or maybe it was simply that he was right and she needed desperately to talk to someone. "I'm in trouble," she admitted.

"I'm here to help. Just to be a sounding board if that's what you need."

She closed her eyes briefly and gave in to her need. "I'm not in trouble the way you're thinking. But

I am in trouble. I think I'm losing my mind. I lost my husband just over two years ago. Before I showed up here in Ransom Creek." She hadn't told anyone since she'd arrived in town and now she wasn't sure whether she should have. And yet, there was also a sense of relief.

Vance had turned onto Main Street and the diner was not far. He braked hard on the deserted street. "You're a *widow*? I...I'm sorry for your loss. You're so *young*. I wasn't expecting that." He shook his head, as if trying to get his head around her revelation. "Are you okay? Of course you aren't—I'm sorry." He slowly drove the short distance to the diner.

Her heart ached. "Thank you. It's been a hard two years. Things are complicated. Things happened and I broke on his death date. I couldn't take it anymore and I ran. And ended up here." She hadn't meant to go that far, to reveal that much but she had.

He pulled into a parking space in front of the diner and rolled the windows down before shutting off the engine and turning to her. The concern in his expression was illuminated from the light coming from the streetlamp next to the diner. Her heart clenched at how much he looked like Mark. And the sympathy she saw in his expressive green eyes dug deep into her soul.

Eyes that belonged only to Vance, she realized.

Mark's had been brown and Vance's were an extraordinary green. Like green glass backlit by fire and reflecting the lamp light.

"What happened to make you run? Too much grief catch up to you?"

His words tightened around her aching heart. "Partly, and there were some circumstances... I...I was responsible for the wreck he died in. I was driving the car and I can't get over it. I can't move forward from that moment. I've been a mess ever since I woke up in the hospital and realized he was gone... I'm sorry I'm telling you this." She was just exposing too much.

"*No*, please don't be sorry. I'm glad you are talking. You need to. I won't break your trust by mentioning it to anyone."

He reached for her arm and placed his hand on her

forearm. The heat burned her skin and spread through her like wildfire. She closed her eyes, fighting the reaction, which wasn't helping the emotions she was struggling with. And yet, there was comfort in his touch. It drew her while at the same time caused her to want to run. She needed to move on. To let go.

"How long were you in the hospital?"

"Just two days. Mark died and I just had a bump on my head from being knocked out. It was horrible. How could he die and I basically walk away unharmed?" Tears stung her eyes again, there was so much that happened that night, but she could not bring herself to talk about that… "I need to go in. I'm sorry. But thank you for the ride. And for not telling anyone. I can't bring myself to talk about any of this right now, and…" She couldn't go on. "I'll see you later."

She opened her door before he could try to stop her and slid out. She closed it behind her and hurried to the sidewalk. Her hand shook as she unlocked the door to the stairs that led up to her apartment. She turned to wave and nearly bumped into him.

"I can't let you go so upset. Are you sure you're okay?"

No. She wasn't okay, but she found an unsettling reassurance in his concern. "Thank you for being so nice." She blinked hard.

"I'm glad you think I am, but that didn't answer my question. Are you okay?"

"Vance, I'm as okay as I'm going to be. I feel oddly like a boat in a raging storm without an anchor. But…I'm going to find my way. Eventually. I think when I ran, that was what I was hoping for. But…"

"Can I hug you? I just feel like you could probably use a hug."

Tears sprang to her eyes and her heart burned with fear, with hope, with need. She had missed Mark's hugs so, so much. Had longed for them.

She nodded, not trusting her voice.

Vance stepped forward and tenderly wrapped her in his strong arms.

He smelled so nice, a light cologne mixed with the lingering scent of soap, sunshine, and maleness. It was intoxicating to her longing senses. But most of all, he felt like strength and kindness all wrapped around her like a security blanket. She eased closer, needing to feel his body next to hers. Something about her heart beating against his startled her, drew her to move even closer to him, to hang on tightly.

He stood very still, letting her move at her own pace. She hesitated then laid her cheek against his shoulder and relaxed into the feel of him.

For just a few moments, she would allow herself to fully feel and relax into this sweet man. His hands caressed her back, easing her tense muscles.

She could stay there forever...

But she had learned that forever didn't exist.

Most of all, she didn't think she deserved thoughts like she was suddenly having about Vance. "I better go in." She forced herself to let go of him.

"Call if you need me." He handed her a card. "That's not my card but I put my number on the back."

She glanced at his big bold scrawl on the back of the card, uncertain how to react. "Thank you." The fact that she wouldn't be calling him was not the issue; it was the fact that he was nice enough to offer.

"I mean it—call any time," he urged.

Her heart skipped a few beats as his sincere eyes bore into her like a torch. She nodded then headed inside to the safety of her apartment while her pulse pounded in her ears.

Her life had just added yet another complication.

Another reason to feel guilty.

CHAPTER SIX

Drake was standing at the corral the next morning when Vance strode out of the house and headed across to talk. Drake had his own place but he stayed at the ranch when he wasn't hauling himself and his horses from one rodeo to another.

Vance had always loved the rodeo and the travel that went hand in hand with it, and he was usually ready to get back on the road. For the first time ever, he realized he wasn't ready to head out on the two-week trip to New Mexico and then on to Denver. He felt restless, unsettled about the thought of leaving, and there was only one person responsible for that feeling. *Libby.*

What if she wasn't here when he returned? What if the pain in her heart and in her eyes that he could see so clearly drove her to run? She was grieving and full of fear—of what, he wasn't completely sure but something. *Was she afraid of facing a future without her husband, or was it something more?* Whatever it was, it had sent her running and she'd shown up here. In his heart of hearts, he couldn't help but think she had arrived in Ransom Creek not by chance, but because she was supposed to.

And his gut told him that if she could find healing anywhere, it would be here among the good people he had always known and who had rallied around him and his siblings during the years they'd adjusted to life without their mother.

She needed to be here.

Drake acknowledged him as Vance reached him. "Was Libby all right? She looked really upset last night."

There wasn't much he could say without breaking

Libby's confidence and he wasn't going to do that. "She's had some hard times. She shared some of it with me and I'm not at liberty to break her confidence, but I'm glad she's here with Gert and Aunt Trudy and Sally Ann around her, not to mention Beth, Jenna, Lori, and Bella. She needs people looking out for her right now."

Drake's lips flattened and his expression was thoughtful. "I thought as much. There is a sadness to her. Women need women for support and they're a good group."

"Yes. Look, Drake, I have to leave on Thursday and I'm worried about leaving her."

"Wow, that happened quick. You're involved."

Vance heard the certainty in Drake's observation. His brother knew how uninvolved he usually was where dating was concerned. Vance had a goal of winning the NFR and hadn't let anything get in the way of that. He dated rarely, a discipline that he had taken on over a year ago, after he realized that a girlfriend required more attention than he could give if he were to stay focused on his goal. But Libby had gotten past the barrier to his well-ordered life.

It was true. "Yeah, I am. I can't seem not to be. I'm going to go see if I can see her today. I think she needs a friend."

Drake studied him hard. "I hope it works out for you."

He felt awkward not being able to discuss this with Drake. Drake was a rock. Always had been, having been the eldest kid. When his dad had come home and broke the tragic news about their mother, Drake had changed in that moment. He'd taken his role seriously and had been there for the rest of them. It was as if his young shoulders had grown strong enough to carry all their pain and grief. They'd had their moments of rebellion against a brother who'd almost become too protective and almost a mini version of their dad. But as an adult, Vance appreciated Drake. And recognized that he'd suffered too, but cowboy'd up and tried to take the load for the rest of them.

He couldn't take this load though, because it wasn't his load to share. He'd promised not to mention Libby's heartbreak to anyone and he wouldn't. Still, knowing his big brother was there for him if he needed him helped.

And he knew he could ask Drake and all of his brothers to watch out for Libby when he left. As much as he was dreading leaving, this knowledge helped. He barely knew Libby but he'd known last night that she was special in his life.

"Look, I need to run some errands before I come out to help work the cattle. Are you heading out now?"

"In an hour. Everyone else just loaded up early. It's a big job but I have some paperwork to finish on a cattle shipment so I can't leave yet. We weren't sure if you were planning on helping today or not since you're leaving in a couple of days."

"No, I'm helping. I wouldn't miss it. I just had a conference call with one of my sponsors and now I need to ride into town and see how Libby's doing this morning."

Drake hitched a brow. "Does she know how much you travel?"

"We haven't gotten that far. But she will. And truth is, I don't know really where we stand. This is all new and complicated. Very complicated, so I don't need you jumping to conclusions."

"Got it. Good luck."

"Thanks." He headed to his truck. He didn't take his time as he turned his truck toward town. Instead, he pressed the gas pedal and hoped Reb, the Ransom Creek sheriff, wasn't sitting on the side of the road somewhere hoping to hand out a speeding ticket.

Libby woke with swollen eyes and a headache. Her mind had not shut down after Vance had dropped her off. Instead, it had swirled with thoughts as she'd fought for footing. *How could this have happened?* She hadn't been forthcoming with everything about that horrible night when Mark died. She just couldn't speak the words. Couldn't admit the marriage she'd believed was fine hadn't been. Even thinking about it made her pulse speed up and her skin to get clammy. Her marriage had failed. And she hadn't even known it until it was too late.

When she'd had the confrontation at Mark's grave

with his mistress nearly two months ago, it had been the last straw, she'd broken and she'd just needed to get away.

She no longer drove since the wreck, so she'd told her cab driver to take her to the bus station. She'd bought a ticket and had ridden to a small town somewhere between Dallas and Houston. She'd gotten off the bus and went into the convenience store to get something for her headache. The older truck driver happened to be looking for some, too, and he'd started talking to her. He'd been kind and asked whether she was okay. Told her she reminded him of his granddaughter and when they'd both paid for their medicine, she'd watched him walk to his truck and had hurried after him and caught a ride.

He was the only reason she'd ended up in this small town, because he was delivering supplies here. Exhausted, confused, and emotionally drained on so many levels that when she got out of the truck and spotted the quaint motel across the street she knew she had to get a room and rest. He'd offered her a ride back if she needed it, but she had no plans to backtrack.

In need of sleep, she'd paid cash for one night. The room had been surprisingly charming and she'd slept for twelve hours. When she'd woken up, she'd walked to Main Street and found the café and had coffee and bacon—to which Miss Gert had added two thick pieces of buttered bread with homemade marmalade. It had been delicious and Libby had sat in the corner and watched the happy crowd as she ate and tried to figure out what she was going to do.

Miss Gert had been attentive, refilling her coffee cup a couple of times. It had been amazing to watch the older woman work. She took care of the entire breakfast rush by herself.

To Libby's surprise, when Miss Gert brought the check, she'd asked whether Libby happened to be looking for a job. Startled, Libby had said yes in a spur-of-the-moment decision. And she'd stayed.

Something about the people here and the job, that she now loved, had held her here. But then Vance had walked in and sent her world spiraling again. She'd very nearly run again right then and there, but Miss Gert had been so nice and said she needed her. She couldn't let the good hearted woman down.

The fact that Vance reminded her so much of Mark had hurt, reminded her every day he was in town of what she had lost…but still, she had not been able to leave.

Until now.

She was getting feelings for Vance. Had even started not having a knee jerk reaction to the resemblance because she now saw Vance as himself. She hated to leave Miss Gert short-handed again, so she dressed and went in to work her scheduled breakfast through lunch shift. Before she left, she'd let her sweet boss know she was leaving. And she might very well leave tomorrow. She just needed to work and sort through her thoughts. Get her thoughts together and make a decision. She wouldn't let herself just run on a whim again.

She was moving slow because she'd not slept well and couldn't get her mind off what had happened between her and Vance the night before. Mark was on her mind too. Her heart was in a very strange place, feeling guilt for not only the accident but also for the feelings that Vance had stirred inside her. Feelings that she hadn't fathomed ever feeling again. She'd felt alive last night when he'd held her in his arms.

She told herself it was just attraction. Vance was overwhelmingly attractive. And yet, this sense that she couldn't wait to see him again was stronger than anything else she was experiencing. And as she went about serving breakfast, she tried so hard not to think about those disturbing feelings.

"The wedding was just beautiful last night, don't you think?" Miss Trudy asked Libby as she set the older woman's coffee down in front of her.

Vance's aunt and Miss Gert and Miss Sally Ann were having breakfast at the back table this morning. Probably to discuss the wedding and who knew, the three might be trying to figure out who they hoped would have the next wedding in town. Libby wouldn't put it past the three ladies to have matchmaking tendencies.

"Didn't you enjoy it?" Miss Sally Ann asked when Libby didn't immediately answer Miss Trudy's question.

"Oh, yes, I did. The food was wonderful. And the wedding was beautiful."

Miss Gert slid into the seat next to Sally Ann. "You were a lifesaver, helping out. Did Vance get you home okay?"

She bit her lip, realizing all three ladies looked very interested in her answer. "Yes, he brought me straight home. I was just feeling tired."

"I think it's lovely that he gave you a lift." Sally Ann casually stirred her coffee. "He is the sweetest young man. And you are just the right age."

Libby's mouth went dry. There was more stirring here than just Sally Ann's coffee.

"And you looked so nice on the dance floor together." Vance's aunt looked unabashedly pleased.

"He's a good dancer." That was all she could think of to say.

"All my boys are," Trudy said. "You two looked perfect together."

She looked at Miss Gert, hoping for help but her eyes were twinkling.

Libby got a sinking feeling. "I better go check on

the orders. I'll be back with yours when they're done."
She had to force herself not to run.

Grady Black walked into the café and took the
seat at the counter. His dark gaze found her and tracked
her as she got behind the counter.

"You sure look pretty today," he said.

Not wanting to encourage him, since it was
obvious he wanted more than eggs and coffee from her
and she was not interested she ignored the compliment.
"Can I take your order?"

He frowned. "Eggs and bacon breakfast and coffee
and maybe you'll stick your finger in it and sweeten it
up for me."

She fought down a frown and kept her expression
neutral. "I'll put this order in and get your coffee." She
put the order on through the window for Hoss, who
was busy at the grill and had his back to her. Then she
grabbed the coffee and a mug and set it on the counter
in front of Grady. He watched her and smiled as she
finished filling the mug. When she started to turn to
put the coffee carafe up he grabbed her wrist. Shocked
she froze and met his gaze. She heard the café door

open but was too busy looking at Grady.

"You didn't put your finger in my coffee," he said, keeping his voice down.

"I'm not going to. Let me go."

"Not till you sweeten my coffee. Or am I not good enough for you? I heard about you and Vance Presley dancing the night away at that fancy wedding they had last night."

She swallowed hard, not wanting to cause a scene she tugged at her hand. "Let go. Its none of your business what I do. I'm not better than anyone."

"Then go out with me," he leaned forward and drew her with the pressure on her arm.

"Let go," she said again, this time a little louder because his hand was hurting her.

In the next instant Grady was yanked backwards off his stool. He let go of her wrist and yelped as he landed, sprawled on his butt on the old wood floor. Vance stood, legs apart glaring down at him.

"What th-" Grady growled.

"You touch her again and you're going to answer to me."

"She's not your property."

"No, she's her own property and she told you to let go of her. Seems to me you shouldn't have been touching her in the first place. Now get up and get out."

Grady wasn't a small cowboy, he was actually larger than Vance, who was lean but muscular and quick on his feet. She had a feeling hanging onto a bucking horse helped build some of that strength.

Grady got up, his expression stormy. "Fine. She's not worth the headache anyway."

The moment the words were out Vance yanked back then slammed him in the jaw, sending the cowboy stumbling back. He ran into a table and a cowboy who'd had his back to them but was now half turned watching the show and pushed Grady off his table.

"You asked for that," he said then picked up his coffee and grinned, looking at the furious Vance to Grady, who was rubbing his jaw.

"You better keep your mouth shut. And remember, you

touch her again, you'll have the whole Presley clan down on you. Now get out of here."

Gert stepped up beside Vance. "And don't come back in here until you apologize and mean it. Otherwise I don't need your business Grady Black."

"Fine. I'm gone."

Libby blinked back maddening tears. Humiliation swamped her. Hoss had come to stand beside her and placed his hand on her shoulder. "I'm sorry. I had just looked out of the window to see him holding you but before I could come out of the kitchen with my baseball bat Vance had taken care of you. You alright, honey?"

"I am."

"Are you sure?" Vance asked coming up and shielding her from the view of many of the customers.

"I'm sure. Thank you. I don't know why he did that?"

Vance frowned. "The cowboy has a chip on his shoulder. He's never liked me or my brothers. But I've never seen him act like that."

"I haven't either," Miss. Gert said. "He just took to

Libby as soon as he saw her but I told him to leave her alone. I guess he decided to ignore me."

"He knew I danced with you at the wedding," she offered. "I think he got jealous."

Vance's frown deepened. "He won't bother you again. I'll inform Reb and he'll have a talk with him. There's no call for any man to manhandle a woman."

"Thank you. I'm fine, so go sit down and I'll take your order. People are staring."

"Fine. But only if you feel like it."

She was not a wilting flower. She pulled her shoulders back and put her hands on her hips. "Please go sit down."

Miss Gert grinned. "I think she means business." With that she walked back to her booth and slid in beside her friends.

Vance took a seat at the counter and Libby forced herself to appear much calmer than she was as she walked back around the counter to face him.

Now that things were calming down she saw that he looked freshly showered, alive, and very much the man she couldn't get off her mind. Even more so now that he'd defended her.

He smiled and her stomach dropped to her toes. *Better her stomach than a plate of food.* He took his hat off, exposing his dark hair and showing off those stunning green eyes. He didn't say anything, thankfully. Just waited for her to say something.

Feeling weak-kneed, she knew everyone was watching them, especially the ladies from the back booth. They were watching like hawks.

"Good morning," she said. "Let's start the morning off again."

He grinned. "Good morning."

"Can I get you some coffee?" She tried to appear calm but was far from it.

"That'd be great. How are you?" He cupped his hands together on the bar and leaned forward as he spoke in quiet tones for her ears only. "Really, how are you?"

She busied herself by grabbing the coffeepot and held on for dear life. She at least might have made it past the dropping dishes when he was around. But after what had just happened she was a little excitable and could very well drop everything. "I'm okay. Really. Thank you again for the ride last night. And for being a sounding board." She poured the coffee and whispered, "I needed it."

"Any time." His smile tickled her insides.

When he wrapped his hands around the warm mug, her thoughts flew to how she'd felt with those hands holding her close, comforting her. She looked up to find him studying her. She had no words.

"How are your knuckles?"

He scowled. "My hand is fine."

She hoped so. "I'd hate for you to injure yourself on my account and not be able to ride."

"You're worth it." He held her gaze, and nodded as if to emphasize how much she was worth.

She blinked away tears again, she cried so much these days it seemed, but if Vance only knew how worthless she'd been feeling since Mark...she swallowed hard and didn't let herself finish the thought. It only caused her pain. She looked at Vance Presley, the man who had a way of making her feel worthy again. The way he was looking at her now, made her feel warm all over. She reached for his hand, a tingle playing through her at touching him. She gave him a gentle pat, remembering they were being watched then let go. "I'll get you come coffee."

He watched as she poured his coffee. "I came in to see if you were okay but to also ask if you might want to go for a ride with me this evening. Do you ride horses? If you don't we could ride a four-wheeler. But, I have to leave in two days for a couple of weeks and I was hoping to spend some time with you."

He wanted to spend time with her. She should say no. She was leaving tomorrow.

You need to try to move forward with your life.

She nodded before words formed. And he smiled like a brilliant sun bursting through cloudy skies. Her world seemed to lift and float for a moment.

His smile burst to life like a flaming star shooting across the night sky. "Good, great. I've got to go help work the cattle and then clean up, so what time do you get off?"

"Three."

"Then I'll be here at five. Give you a couple of

hours to be off your feet while I help vaccinate a lot of cows today."

"Five is good." She'd take whatever he offered.

"I'll see you then. I better go, so the brothers don't call me a slacker." He chuckled and laid a five on the counter—for the coffee and a tip, she assumed—then he put his hat back on and strode to the door and outside without a backward glance.

He'd never taken even a sip of his coffee. If certain people weren't watching, she'd have downed the hot brew herself and hoped it helped settle her nerves. She was going riding with Vance Presley. And she felt like she was walking on air.

But you're leaving tomorrow.

The reminder of her plans hit her. She could change her mind. Leave later. She shelved the subject and went back to work because, especially after the way he'd come to her rescue she couldn't just leave tomorrow and leave him hanging. That would just be wrong.

Besides that, she was excited about something for the first time in years.

CHAPTER SEVEN

By the time five o'clock slowly, slowly rolled around, Libby had talked herself out of the outing at least ten times. And talked herself right back into it just as many because she really wanted to spend time with Vance.

By the time he knocked on her door, she practically ran down the stairs to meet him.

"Hey," he said, his gaze warming at the sight of her and that knowledge alone did something wonderful to her spirits. "You ready?"

She nodded and followed him to the truck. She

had no idea if she was ready or not but again, there was the fact that she couldn't help herself. She wanted to spend time with Vance.

He'd been in the saddle all day long, so he'd suggested they take the ATV but he promised to take her horseback riding when she told him she'd once loved to ride. At the moment, she was loving the ATV option since she was holding him around the waist as they raced across the pasture and it was a delightful feeling.

The wind in her face and the late afternoon sun on her skin made her feel alive in a way she hadn't felt in a very long time. And the feel of this wonderful man in her arms had something to do with it too.

The guilt and sadness that hovered around her like a constant cloud had been left somewhere behind them on the rutted trail.

"Are you enjoying yourself?" Vance asked over his shoulder as they approached the top of a hill.

"I am. I love the speed." She laughed when he shot her a grin.

"I do too. I'm a bit of an adrenaline junky."

"But you don't like rock climbing?" she asked, remembering his funny question from the night before.

He slid the ATV to a halt at the top of the hill. "Nope, not a fan of that. But I get my thrills other ways. I guess that's why I never get tired of riding broncs." His gaze met hers before he studied the pasture below them.

She could have stared at his profile all day, but followed the direction he was looking and gasped. There were horses everywhere.

"Our wild Mustang herd," he said, obviously understanding her gasp.

"They're gorgeous."

"Yes, they are. I love watching them. We're having an adoption two weeks after I get back from Colorado. You should come."

"But they look so happy here."

"They are. But we take them on, train some of them to be cow ponies, and others we adopt out. We can't take them all, but we can do our part in helping others who want to give a home to an American wild Mustang. And some want them to ride."

"I think that's kind of sad, taking a wild Mustang and putting a saddle on it."

"Yeah, it is sad to some extent. There's a lot of controversy out there about it. And everyone just has to have their own opinion. I look at it as a reality. We and others like us are taking on as many as we can in order to keep them from starving or being killed in government roundups."

She gasped. "They kill them?"

"It's been done. And it wasn't good. And now there's a chance the Land Management Bureau might get the okay to do it again. But there's two sides to the story and I get that. One side wants to make sure the Mustangs remain healthy and they need to be managed, but I'm never an advocate for eradication. There has to be better answers. There are a few nonprofits working desperately to find solutions. I went out there last year to help them for a little while. They're trying things like birth control to slow the breeding down."

"How are they doing that? If the horses are wild, how can they get close to them?"

"One group is testing dart guns that shoot birth control instead of sedatives. It could help. In the meantime, ranchers like us take on as many horses as we can and help get them adopted out. We also break as many as we can and still keep up with the ranch working."

"I'm getting it now. So, I'm assuming you help break them. I mean, since you ride saddle broncs."

He chuckled. "I do help, but we don't break them like that. We gentle break them. It's a process. They're terrified when we start and we have to take our time and earn their trust. Sometimes bucking is involved. However, it's not something we want."

"I'd like to see that sometime." She loved listening to him talk. She could tell he had a passion for the horses and she'd at first believed he was all about the rodeo. Which was fine—he was obviously great at it; still, this new aspect of him made her like him even more.

He turned so he could look at her better. "If you want to watch a horse being taught to trust, then come out tomorrow. I'm going to be working with one before I leave."

She was tempted, but she was leaving.

"You'll enjoy it. I promise," he said when she hesitated.

She could leave the day after tomorrow. The same day he left to go to his rodeo. "I'd like that very much and I'm not scheduled to work, so it would be great." Excitement rushed through her. It had been so long since she'd had anything to really look forward to. She certainly wasn't looking forward to leaving. But, suddenly, she was not only anticipating watching Vance work with his horses; she now was anticipating spending her day off with him.

His lip hitched, sending butterflies flying through her. "I'm picking you up early. Horse breaking takes all day."

She laughed. "I can handle it."

"I'm sure you can." His eyes twinkled then grew serious. "Libby, you've handled so much on your own. I think you're incredible. And I'm not even sure if that's something I should say because what you've been through is so painful for you."

"It was…very hard." Her throat hurt as emotion ambushed her. It did that at the most unexpected times lately. And lately, it seemed almost as if it showed up more than when the wreck first happened and her world fell apart, learning that Mark had died. She blinked hard and took a steadying breath.

"I'm sorry. I didn't mean to make you cry." He slid from the four-wheeler and took her hand. "Come here."

She swung her legs to the ground and moved into the warmth of his waiting embrace. "I seem to be more emotional these days and I don't mean to be. I mean, I ran—I was so upset before and now I'm here. And panic keeps waylaying me."

"Are you going to run again or stay and face your fears?"

His soft words washed over her. "I don't…" She looked up at him, a light dawning, and she changed what she'd been about to say. "Do you think that's what I've been doing? I mean to be honest I was actually thinking of leaving soon."

He held her tightly with one arm and gently traced

the line of her face in a soothing caress. "Please don't. I do believe you are running from something. You remind me of a Mustang that's been through a tough loss of everything its known and having to learn to adjust to its new reality. I think, and believe me I'm no therapist, but I think you've reached a turning point in your life and you know it's time to face your new reality. That maybe you're emotional because you're internally understanding that you need to move forward...not keep hiding or running."

His words hit targets inside her. She pulled away and turned to look out at the horses. *Was that what she'd been doing? Running from facing the future without Mark?* "What made you say that?" she asked, as he moved to stand next to her.

"When I was a boy and my mom died, I hid in the barn. I'll never forget how mad I was. Or how lost I felt. We were all little. And my dad had to try to keep us all together and tend to a ranch and a new baby. I was hurting too much in my own world to care about all of that. I was hard on Aunt Trudy, too, when she came to stay with us. It took me several years to really move past my mom dying. I was running—I was a little kid but I remember the day I realized it was time to start being happy again."

She couldn't imagine how hard it must have been on him and his siblings when their mother died. "Did you just decide to be happy and it worked?"

The horses were milling around and she loved watching them. It helped calm her while this conversation was risking raising her stress level as it hit so close to home.

He took her hand. "Let's walk. I need to move."

They walked slowly along the ridge instead of toward the horses. There were trees ahead, beautiful old oak trees that had probably been on this land for a hundred years.

"It took some time. It's not like you throw a switch and the happy light comes on. I had my days—in our own ways, all of us were going through different stages of grieving and moving on with our lives. I'd have to remind myself that I'd decided it was time to be happy. But, see, I had a load no one else had. I was mad at my mom when she left for the hospital. I was barely three and the strongest memory I have of my mother is her hugging me while I tried to get out of her arms because I was mad that she wouldn't let me go to the hospital with them."

His words cut deep into her heart at the feelings she felt. *She and Mark had been arguing.* "You were a baby. Your mother understood that."

"I know. But it took me a long time to know that my mother knew I loved her and didn't die thinking I was mad. In reality, she was fighting for her life so she might not have even been thinking about her baby boy, much less about him being angry. A little boy in pain couldn't rationalize those emotions…as a teenager, I couldn't either. I had some tough times and bucking it out on a saddle bronc seemed to give me a semi-safe place to help me work through my demons."

Libby stopped walking and tugged at his hand to halt him. "Your mother was thinking about you. She had to have been thinking about all of her boys and your dad and her new sweet baby girl who she wasn't going to get to raise. You need to remember that and not tell yourself she wasn't. That does her an injustice.

Your guilt about being mad at her is misplaced." Anger at him pulsed through her, stronger than it should have been but she couldn't stop the anger from coming out in her voice.

He cocked his head to the side. "Why does that make you so mad?"

She paused, startled by her outburst and his gaze drilling into her. "Because, I just feel like you're being too hard on yourself and your mom." *And you're being too hard on yourself.*

No, her guilt wasn't misplaced. She was an adult and she'd been really angry.

She yanked her anger back. "And I'm not angry. Just worried. It came out sounding wrong. I don't get angry." *Not with others, anyway.* She stayed neutral. Calm and cool because anger with others could lead to tragedy and she couldn't cause any more pain.

"You were angry."

Panic clutched at her throat. "No." She didn't do anger any more. Anger brought fear with it. She didn't want something to happen to Vance and then she would only remember that she had been angry. And his family would blame her.

And rightly so.

"No, really, I wasn't. Please, you just need to give yourself grace."

"I have. Those are good words. My pastor on the rodeo circuit helped me realize I needed to let it all go and just remember how much love I feel for my mom and how much she felt for me. When I started thinking of that, I stopped struggling with it and truly did give myself grace. I was just telling you how I used to feel. Because I'm wondering if you have something like that going on yourself."

She stepped back. "No, I..." she stuttered, then stopped herself.

"Are you sure? What happened the night of your wreck?"

Vivid memories of that night flashed through her mind. She crossed her arms tightly. "I don't want to talk about it. It was a horrible night."

"I understand that. But obviously it is still haunting you. Driving you to run, to not completely let yourself live today. If there is one thing that I keep in my heart from losing my mom, it's that life is precious and isn't to be taken for granted. Living in the past isn't good for anyone. You can't help anyone if you're stuck in time."

"But what if I can't let go?" *Had she really said that?*

"I think you ran this time because you knew you needed to let go."

She stared at him. Her heartbeat thudded like mud-caked boots clomping on stairs. "I think I'm ready to go back to my apartment." She turned and started to walk back toward the four-wheeler.

"You're running again," he called.

She halted and spun back to face him. He was still standing where she'd left him. "I am not. I just want to leave." He looked disappointed but she didn't address that. "I just need to go home."

"You just need to give yourself some of that grace for whatever it is that is troubling you."

She forced a smile. "I'm fine. Could you take me home now, please?"

His lips flattened into a firm line as he made a

move to follow her.

Good.

She had to hold onto him as they headed back over the pastures. The quietness of the ride gave her plenty of time to fight with herself about her attitude and taking her emotions out on Vance.

When he pulled next to the barn, where the truck was parked, it felt strained between them.

"Vance, I didn't mean to put you off like that. I'm fine. I'm not comfortable talking about all of that."

"I get it. I didn't mean to pry. I just thought since you gave me advice, I would do the same."

He had a point. She'd not even hesitated to offer her thoughts to him. "I should have kept my mouth shut. Your life is your business. I'm sorry."

He frowned. "I didn't mind, Libby. It was actually nice that you cared enough to point out what I needed to do."

Her knees turned to pudding. *He thought she cared.*

His eyes twinkled. "Do you care?"

Yes. "I…of course I do. You're a nice guy." She

tried to look nonchalant but she was far from it.

"Glad you think so. Come on, I'll take you home because I'm coming to pick you up at seven." He smiled and opened the truck door for her.

"Thank you," she said as he waited for her to slide into the seat.

"My pleasure." He smiled and closed the door.

She watched him stride quickly around the front of the big truck. The cowboy completely disarmed her with his charm. His smile. His eyes.

And he'd done it from the first time he walked into the diner, reminding her so much of Mark. But now, he did it because he was him. He might resemble Mark but he wasn't like her late husband, who had been funny and sweet. But Vance had a kindness in him that was undeniable.

And she was drawn to that like a deer to spring water.

"I'll be ready," was all she could say even though every fiber in her body was telling her to run.

CHAPTER EIGHT

"What he's doing now is building trust with the horse. See how the Mustang is pulling back against the bridle with its head and looks terrified?" Marcus Presley explained.

Libby had been surprised to see Vance's dad and his brother Drake at the round pen when she and Vance arrived at the ranch the next morning. They had given her a warm welcome and then Vance went into the arena, where he had a Mustang tied to a post in the middle of the arena. She had been so interested in watching the gentle way he approached the horse and how he used a long fishing pole-looking stick to touch the horse on one side and then the other.

"And this helps the horse?" she asked.

"It does," Drake said from the other side of his dad. "They naturally spook. And their instinct is to run. They have to build the trust with Vance and realize he's not out to harm them."

Marcus nodded. "The pole and Vance moving to one side and the other lets the horse see him and feel him. And also is teaching the horse to move where Vance wants him to move when he lightly touches him on his flanks. That will help when Vance finally rides him this afternoon."

"This afternoon? But he just started. He'll be able to ride already later today?"

"Probably." Drake grinned, a devastating smile that turned his usual serious handsome face into a breathtaking whammy of a face.

Marcus Presley had marked his sons, each in a distinctive way and highlighted with those green eyes. Though Vance was leaner, more playful in his expressions, the smiles were similar...and Vance's smile did much to shake her up inside.

"That's why we're here," Drake continued. "Vance has a gift. Horses respond quickly to him."

Marcus agreed. "He's a trust builder, I like to say."

Their words startled Libby. She had quickly trusted him. And she was prone to run also. *Was he working his magic on her?*

"I find this fascinating. I guess I expected him to jump on the poor horse's back and ride it until it was all bucked out." She shrugged when both his dad and brother smiled at her. Then she laughed. "You can tell I know very little about the world of horses." She had ridden horses but they were already broken. The horses the girls' ranch had were old and so saddle broke, there was no spunk left in them to get the least bit unruly.

Marcus patted her shoulder. "That's okay. We're glad you're here and interested. That's how it begins. You have a look in your eyes that says you're almost hooked. I'm sure Vance would be happy to teach you to ride when he gets home in two weeks."

He was going to be gone two weeks. She'd been thinking about that and knew she would miss him. But maybe while he was gone, she could get her thoughts sorted out. She'd dreamed of the wreck last night. It was never a good night when the nightmare came. But rather than put her into a depression, she'd been happy knowing that Vance was picking her up and giving her something new and exciting to focus on.

Yes, her thoughts were a big mish-mash of emotions. But today she was watching a gorgeous man with his horses and enjoying getting to know Marcus and Drake better.

A truck pulled to a stop near the ranch house and Beth Presley hopped from the driver's seat. She waved then hurried their way.

"She looks like a woman on a mission," Drake said, a smile in his voice.

Marcus chuckled. "Maybe she's going to try to talk you boys into posing with her little goats for that calendar she has planned for y'all."

Libby bit back a smile at the way Drake's serious brows bent together.

"Nope, I made myself clear about that. Not happening."

"She's persistent. I think she believes she's going to wear them all down," Marcus said to Libby. "Have you seen her goats?"

"No, but I've heard of them. They sound adorable."

"Hey, fellas. And Libby, so good to see you. I wasn't expecting to find another female out here."

She gave Marcus and Drake hugs while she talked then smiled at Libby.

"I came to watch Vance tame a horse. Or break a horse," she corrected because what he was doing didn't seem like breaking.

"Gotcha. It is amazing to watch. I'm glad you're here. You can come too. I came to remind you fellas that we're grilling burgers out on the new deck this evening and didn't want you men to forget. Libby, please come, too. I'm sure Vance will be glad to give you a lift."

Vance strode over. "Hey, Beth. I'm coming out to your place tonight and I'd love to give you a ride, Libby," he said, having heard the last of the conversation.

"Great. Since it's partly to celebrate my new deck Cooper built and also a get-together with you since we won't see you for a couple of weeks. And also Lana and Cam before they head home too. Jenna and Shane won't be there, of course, but we can enjoy a small family gathering."

Libby was excited to be included. She really liked Beth and had wanted to see the little goats that Beth dressed up in clothes and used for her calendar business. "If you don't mind, I'd love to come."

"There, it's settled. We're planning on eating around six, though y'all come out any time you get ready."

"Sounds good." Vance looked pleased as his gaze locked on Libby. "Are you enjoying the training lesson? I'm sure Dad and Drake are giving you all the details."

"I am. It's really interesting. It makes me want to learn how to do it."

"I could teach you." He grinned and she had no doubt he could at least try.

Beth nudged her elbow. "You should take him up

on it. Aren't you going to be in town for a few weeks when you get home next time?"

He nodded. "If I do well these next two, I should be able to take a little time to be home to help with the roundups. We could do a little training."

He looked expectantly at her and she made a decision to stay in town a little longer. "Okay, if you have some time."

His eyes twinkled. "Darlin', I'll make time."

They took a break for lunch, and to her surprise, Vance had made up a picnic basket of simple ham sandwiches, chips, and homemade pie that he informed her he'd made himself. That had been a big surprise, but it was all in a picnic basket. He'd carried it out to the four-wheeler and they'd driven a short distance to a creek. A large flat rock protruded out into the path of the creek, making the water have to divert around it. He spread out a thick blanket and they sat in the peaceful spot and ate their lunch.

"I love my family but I figure they'll be around

this evening and there isn't much alone time while I'm in the arena with the horse and you're standing at the fence."

She was in awe of their surroundings and that he'd thought of taking this break and bringing her here. "I love this spot."

"I thought you might. I have spent a lot of time through the years here. It's a good place to think, with the gurgle of the water and the sounds of the woods."

"I can see why you would want to come here."

"It's a good place to fish for small bass, too." His smile was infectious and she smiled back at him.

"That pie looks delicious. What is it?"

"That is chocolate peanut butter surprise. It's one of my specialties."

"Yum. I can't wait to try it. I'm blown away that you like to bake pies. I do too. My favorite is coconut cream, and I love apple crisp and rhubarb too."

"Oh man, pie is my weakness. You should make some of those for the café. Does Gert know you love to bake pies?"

She took a bite of her sandwich. Then watched as

he removed the top piece of bread, laid four potato chips on the ham before replacing the bread, gave it a gentle press before picking up the sandwich and taking a big bite.

Her brows dipped. "Is that good?"

Though he was chewing, he smiled and nodded. After he'd swallowed, he held his sandwich out to her. "This is the only way to eat a mayonnaise and ham sandwich. Take a bite. You'll fall in love."

She hesitated.

"Seriously, I didn't bite that side. Take a bite. Or try it on your own—you won't be sorry."

She leaned forward and bit into his sandwich. The crunchy chips added flavor to the sandwich. "I see what you mean. I think I'll add those to mine."

"Yup, you can eat chips and sandwich separately or together and that right there is the better way."

She placed her chips on her sandwich. "I think you are a kid at heart."

"Is that a bad thing?"

"No, not at all." She kind of needed a little of that in her own life. "I like it."

They didn't speak for a moment, just looked at each other, and then they both took a bite of their sandwiches.

When they were finished, he pulled out the individually wrapped pieces of the firm pie and handed her a piece.

"I hope you like chocolate and peanut butter."

"I love it. This has my mouth watering." And it was so good. "This tastes similar to a peanut butter cheesecake. But better, richer."

"Cream cheese is part of the recipe. I'm glad you like it."

"When do you find time to bake?"

"It relaxes me. I have a small kitchen in my living quarters of my horse trailer and it helps me destress before events. Also makes me have a lot of cowboy friends on the rodeo circuit. They call me the cooking cowboy." He laughed. "Not the most macho title but it's okay with me."

The man was full of surprises. "When you come home, I'll bake a pie for you."

"That sounds like a most excellent idea. Better yet,

what if we bake together?"

Her stomach wobbled and felt bottomless. "I'd like that."

His gaze grew serious. "So, you'll be here when I come home?"

What had happened to her plan to run? "Yes."

"That makes me happy. I hope it makes you happy."

Did it? If she was truthful, she'd say yes and then fight off the niggling voice that hissed she had no right to feel any happiness.

That afternoon, she waited in the large living room of the ranch house while Vance jogged up the stairs to take a quick shower before going to Cooper and Beth's. She found herself wandering around the large space, looking at all the photos of them growing up. There were photos of his mother too. A beautiful brunette with pale blue eyes that were a complete contrast to the vivid green eyes they had inherited from their dad. Vance would have been just as handsome with either color, she realized, considering both were striking and unusual.

There were several action shots of him on the back of broncs in competition, fully decked out in his long-sleeved shirt with sponsorship patches everywhere, deep-toned chaps and spurs as he held one hand up and rode. In some photos, he was fully stretched out and back, and others, his knees seemed almost to touch his ears in the familiar way bronc riders worked their legs up and down as if riding a very wild seesaw. There were also several of him standing in the arena, waving his hat to the crowd and smiling as if he were on top of the world.

The cowboy had charisma and she had no doubt the crowd had been cheering him on. She realized that she would love to see him compete.

The thought came out of nowhere. Her own adrenaline had kicked in, just looking at the photos of him. She was trying her best not to let him in past carefully constructed barriers but he was impossible to ignore.

He jogged down the stairs, grinning, and sent her pulse skittering in all directions, like a puppy sliding on a frozen pond.

"I feel good. That shower was just what I needed." He came close and leaned toward her. "Do I smell better? I hope so. I'm figuring anything is better than sweat and horse."

She laughed, getting a quick whiff of that clean soap and light cologne that he wore. He smelled amazing. "You don't smell like a horse, I can assure you."

"Great. Now let's head that way. I want to get you in the pen with the goats."

"But I need to clean up too."

He leaned in and almost touched her neck with his nose as he breathed her scent in. "You smell great to me."

She could barely breathe, feeling his warm breath against her skin and then, when he pulled back, saw that mischievous glint in his eyes.

"Sorry, I probably shouldn't have done that. But you do smell great."

She sighed internally, feeling every part of her wilt with the threat of fainting. *The man did not—or maybe he did—know the power of his personality. His person…*

She did talk him into running her back to her place and she jogged up the stairs and practically threw herself into a hot shower. She had no fancy soaps, no perfume, barely any lotion but at least the soap she'd bought at the grocery store had a faint floral scent.

And why was she worrying about how she smelled?

She ignored the question and dried off, then hurried into the bedroom and pulled a pair of colored jeans from the pile on the chair where she'd neatly folded all the clothes several women had given her. She felt bad not letting them know that back home she had closets of clothes but there was no way she was contacting anyone and having them sent here. She wasn't ready to let anyone know where she was. She might not ever be ready.

She was tempted to let the life she had go and to just start over. Here as Libby Smith.

Now was not the time to think about that. But while Vance was gone, she had some decisions to make.

CHAPTER NINE

"Yay, I'm so glad you came," Beth squealed as Libby climbed out of Vance's truck. She set the platter she was holding on the table and jogged down the steps to give Libby a hug. "I so hoped you would come."

Libby was completely taken aback at Beth's enthusiastic welcome. "Th-thanks for inviting me."

"Sure, certainly. It's good to see you getting out of the café and mingling. All the girls were excited that you might show up. The guys, too, but you know—they're guys." She laughed and linked her arm through

Libby's. "Excuse us while I take this young lady to the kitchen where the others are busy getting things ready. You might help Trip make sure Cooper isn't burning the burgers, please."

They walked up the steps to a great new deck. It was very wide and had a lot of colorful seating to sit in and enjoy the pretty backyard. Cooper and Trip—one of their best friends, Libby had heard—were busy putting beef patties on the large grill. Libby took a moment to glance toward the barn and spotted several heads peeking over a fence connected to it.

The goats. How fun. They'd had goats at the girls' ranch and she'd loved watching their antics. "I love your deck. But are those your famous goats?"

Beth laughed. "Thanks. I love the deck too. And yes, those are my sweeties. You'll have to go see them in a bit. They're a hoot."

"That would be fun."

"Hi, Libby. We're glad you joined us." Cooper waved his large grilling spatula. "I hope you like burgers."

"I do."

"Perfect." Cooper then pointed his spatula at Vance. "I know he does."

"We're glad you're here, too," Trip said. "Lori was all grins when she heard you might be coming with Vance. It's pretty much a first, you know. The man don't date." He said the last words in a teasing manner, using bad grammar.

Libby would have laughed if the information hadn't sunk in immediately. *Vance didn't date? Why?* "Oh, this isn't a date. I just…" She paused, not sure whether she should have just let the mistake ride or maybe not have tried to correct it.

"She's right, fellas—no date. Just a friend bringing a friend to hang out with his family and friends."

There was a moment of silence then Cooper grinned. "Sounds like a good place to start."

Beth whisked Libby into the kitchen.

Lori Jensen was slicing tomatoes at the kitchen island and greeted her with a big hello and a smile. "It's about time someone got you out of that café and your apartment. And it's Vance who's done it. I thought there was something there the first time I was in the diner and you dropped the plates. He is a cutie."

Everyone was assuming they were dating. The uncomfortable situation put her in an awkward spot. Especially here with his family and best friends.

"They're not dating," Beth said for her. "But we can always hope."

"I'm for that." Lori grinned.

The screen door opened and Lana came through. "Room for another woman?"

"Lana, of course. Oh, you didn't need to bring anything," Beth said when she saw Lana was holding a bowl of potato salad.

"I kind of did it for me. I had a huge and sudden craving for it, so I raided Dad's pantry after me and Cam got in from helping with the cattle vaccinating and whipped some up. Doing it myself enabled me to sneak a small bowl already."

The room had gone quiet as Beth and Lori studied her.

"You went out and helped with the vaccinations?" Lori asked. "You're visiting."

Lana laughed. "The best way to get quality time in

with my brothers and my dad is to work with them. Besides, I have always enjoyed it. What I never enjoyed was them meddling in my life."

"Are you pregnant?" Beth broke in, her words quiet but with a smile in them.

Lana looked startled and guilty.

Suddenly, Libby remembered how tired Lana had been at the wedding reception and that she'd been pale. Now having cravings for certain foods. It made sense.

"Are you?" Lori gasped, setting her knife on the chopping block and wiping her hands off as she came around to where the rest of them stood.

Lana grimaced but her eyes sparkled happily. "Okay, I am. But we haven't announced it yet. I was actually planning on doing it later this evening, after Dad and Drake got here. And we didn't want to announce it before the wedding because that was Jenna and Shane's time to shine."

There was a short stampede as Beth and Lori moved to Lana and threw their arms around her.

Libby was happy for her.

Later, after Drake and Marcus had arrived and

everyone was finishing their meal, Lana and Cam shared their news with the men. Libby enjoyed seeing Vance's jaw drop and then he whooped really loud as another stampede ensued and the brothers engulfed their sister and slapped Cam on the back in congratulations. It was a very happy moment. A first for the family, as this would be the first grandchild for Marcus.

"Your mother would have loved this," he told Lana, kissing her forehead then hugging her tight. Emotion was raw on his face and it hit Libby hard as she realized that all these years later he still hurt.

And shouldn't it be so for those you love? She thought so. *And hadn't they said that the pretty lady he'd brought to the dance was the first person he'd dated in all those years?* At least the only person anyone knew about, she'd heard someone in the diner speculating.

When things had died down, Vance took her elbow. "Want to go see the goats before it gets dark?"

"I'd love to." *Be alone with you.* The words rang through her mind and she was glad she hadn't accidently said them out loud.

"We'll be back. We have a date with some cute little gals and a few ugly little fellas down by the barn."

"Don't call my babies ugly," Beth called with laughter bubbling in her words.

"Sorry." Vance grinned at Libby. "She falls for that every time. I like to tease her."

"Funny." She elbowed him and he grunted, though she'd barely touched him. "Showboat."

He slipped his arm over her shoulder, a casual movement that seemed a natural reaction as he tugged her into the crook of his arm as they walked. "I've had fun today. I just want you to know."

She met his gaze. "Me too," she admitted.

The goats were waiting. There were four of them. And they pranced and danced and hopped and jumped as if they were unable to stop their erratic antics. She laughed and when Vance opened the gate and led the way inside with them, she immediately bent to pet them. Immediately, all four small goats bombarded her, causing her to lose her balance and she fell back with one in her arms. Both she and Vance were laughing as the little goat did a tap dance on Libby's chest.

"Hang on." Vance chuckled as he scooped the kid off her and set it to the side. He reached down for her hand and tugged her up. "That was an adventure. You okay?"

"I'm great. They are balls of energy."

"Are you ready to go?" he asked.

"Whenever you are. I'm assuming you're heading out very early in the morning."

He pushed a piece of hair from her face and plucked a strand of hay from her shirt. "I am. Actually, about five at the latest. I have a long way to go."

"Then I'm ready. I've had a great time. And hearing Lana and Cam's announcement was really a treat."

"Yeah, I can't believe I'm going to be an uncle."

"You'll be an amazing uncle."

He stared at her. "You think so?"

"I know so. How could you think otherwise?"

"Oh, I'm planning to work really hard at it. Though being on the road so much will limit my being around them. I hope I get to see the baby enough."

"Do you travel a tremendous amount?"

"Yeah, I do. But I have to be honest with you, Libby. This is the first time I've ever not been raring to get back out there. Competition and scores drive me. To make it to the national finals, it takes scores. The best scores, and that takes hauling across the country and competing and winning."

Her spirits sank—why, she wasn't sure. It wasn't as if she were planning to have a relationship with him. She had somehow managed to pull her way out of the dark hole she'd been in for several months and she believed it was Vance who had helped her. But life on the road like that seemed hard. Especially if he were married.

"Is that why you don't date?"

He leaned his head back and smiled. "Who told you that?"

She bit her lip. "People. Okay, your sisters-in-law. Not that I asked."

"Oh, I wouldn't mind if you had asked."

She chuckled and knew she was going to miss him

while he was gone.

They walked to the porch and said their good-byes. He hugged his sister and told her to take care of herself and then congratulated Cam again.

"Thanks," Cam said. "I'm thrilled and I know when we tell my family, there is going to be a big celebration in Windswept Bay. This baby is going to have more uncles and aunts than most babies."

Vance wore a comical expression. "Yeah, with your big family and ours, it's going to be huge. This kid will rack up at birthdays and Christmas."

"True." Cam laughed. "But it will be loved. And that's what matters."

"That's all that matters," Vance said. "Do you have any brothers or sisters?" Vance asked as they got in the truck and headed toward town.

She folded her hands in her lap and thought of his lovely family. And the new baby and how it had to feel so wonderful to belong to such a large family. "No. I was raised on a ranch for girls. It was a foster care facility."

"Your whole life?" he looked through the dark cab

at her.

"I lost my parents early and was there until I turned eighteen."

"I'm sorry."

"It was okay. I had animals and the housemother was nice. It wasn't an ideal situation but better than some."

"You have a great attitude. I'm glad you're okay."

Was she okay?

When they arrived back at her apartment, she hesitated at her door. She had the strongest urge to invite him up for a moment and fought not to. He leaned against the doorframe as she slipped the key in. Her heart was heavy as she thought about him being gone for two weeks. Just two days ago, she had been ready to run and now she was sad that he was leaving and she was going to wait for him.

"Do you have any coffee up there?" he asked, quietly.

Her stomach churned. "I do. Will it keep you up?"

What a crazy thing to say.

"It might, but I can handle it if it gives me a little more time alone with you."

Their gazes locked and she couldn't move. "Okay." The word slipped out. And she opened the door and led the way up the stairs. She was very aware of him walking close behind her. Very aware of every step his boots made on the wooden stairs. When she made it to the landing, she was thankful that she'd straightened up that morning. "It's a tiny space."

"I don't need much space. That looks like a comfortable couch." He was standing close and she was so aware of him.

Needs and desires that she'd shut down and not let herself think about swept through her. She took a step away from him. "I'll make the coffee." She hurried away and fumbled with preparing the coffee. He sat down on the small love seat that had been in the apartment for who knew how long. She'd vacuumed the stuffing out of it when she had found an ancient but strong vacuum in one of the closets.

When she finished getting the machine going, she

walked around the tiny counter that separated the space. He patted the seat beside him. Feeling weak in every aspect of her body, she moved toward him. *What was she doing?* She hesitated then took the hand he held out to her and she sank down into the small space beside him.

His arm was across the back of the love seat and she sank next to him. Her heart thumped as she found herself pressed close to his body.

"Don't be worried." He shifted to face her better. The movement brought her closer to him as his arm slipped off the back of the love seat and gently draped around her shoulders. His beautiful green eyes searched hers. She could hardly breathe as she soaked up the feel of being next to him. In his arms, wanting him to kiss her so badly that it was a physical pain.

"I'm trying so hard not to kiss you," he said. "You are so lovely. And I'm going to miss you while I'm gone."

She nodded. Everything rushed around her as her gaze rested on his lips and his hand made gentle circles on her back, putting ever so slight pressure to bring her closer to him. *There were so many reasons for her to tell him to leave. So many reasons kissing him was all wrong.* But as she looked at him, she wasn't in the reasoning mood. She wanted, needed to feel the touch of his lips against hers now. And without thinking any more about it, she leaned forward and kissed him.

CHAPTER TEN

She was kissing him. Vance had hoped she would sit with him on the couch and maybe, if he could win her trust, she might snuggle with him a bit. But he'd never dreamed she would kiss him. Oh, he'd thought about it all evening. But a guy could have his dreams. For them to come true so unexpectedly was more than he'd fathomed. So startled was he that for the first instant that she pressed her lips to his, he froze. Her lips were warm and trembled against his as her palms flattened on his chest. His heart thundered in his ears. It registered that her kiss paused and she was pulling back.

Finally coming to his senses, he pulled her close and brought his lips to hers. She sighed against his lips and sank into him and he was home. She felt right. Her soft, warm lips pulled emotions, and longing and aching need, from him. He needed her here like this always.

He deepened the kiss, losing his head for a moment and then he came to his senses. *What was he doing?* And as if she came to hers in that very moment, she jumped back from him and her hand went to her lips. Her expression was dazed. Her eyes almost glazed. She shook her head and then bolted to her feet and moved to the kitchen.

"Coffee. I need a cup. Do you still want one?" Her voice broke as she yanked a cabinet open and clasped a mug in her hand. It was the same kind they used in the café. She set it on the counter then pressed her hands flatly on the counter, her head dropped and her shoulders drooped. He knew what she was feeling. He rose on legs that felt rubbery and moved to stand behind her.

"I'm sorry. I didn't mean to cross a line."

She laughed mirthlessly. "I crossed the line. What was I thinking?"

"That you needed a kiss." He hadn't meant it to sound so blunt but she sounded as if kissing him was the end of the world. "Libby, what are you afraid of? Moving forward? Or of me?"

"Both." She turned and her beautiful eyes were bright. "I'm scared."

He stepped forward and cupped her face. "Please don't be scared of me. I'll give you all the time you need, darlin'. Maybe me being gone two weeks is a good thing. You feel something for me. I feel something for you. But I want you to be ready before we mess this up by moving too fast. So, relax. I'll move at your speed."

"Okay. I kissed you. I didn't mean to. I just couldn't help myself."

He smiled. "I'm glad. Now, take care of yourself while I'm gone. Please call me if you need anything. If Grady bothers you in any way you call me or one of my brothers. Call for any reason. Promise me."

"I promise. Be safe. And I'm sorry I'm such a mess."

"You're perfect. And you're going to be all right. If there is one thing I've learned, it's people grieve at different rates. And moving forward also has no set timetable."

She inhaled sharply. Then smiled sadly. "It's complicated."

He ran his hand across her jaw. "I hope when I get back maybe you can trust me enough to share your complications with me."

She nodded. "I'll try."

He bent forward and brushed his lips gently across hers—swift, brief—and then he headed toward the door.

"Vance," she called and he turned. "Thank you. Good luck."

He grinned. "Then I should be on top of the leader board because I've never felt luckier than I do right now." He waved then opened his truck door. "Libby, you're going to be here when I get back, right?"

Her palms clammed up and she felt unsteady as

she relaxed against the door frame, pretending to be calm. "Yes. I'll be here."

The next week passed with the speed of a turtle with short legs.

"I tell you what, I'm going to get my gun and shoot that skunk if it doesn't stop coming by here. I keep hoping it will move on but the rascal waddled out from under my storage building when I went out to grab some more supplies this morning. Nearly sprayed me—would have if I hadn't froze to the spot while he calmed down and then headed off into the vacant lot out there."

They were sitting at a booth, filling salt and pepper shakers and folding napkins. It was three o'clock and their slowest time. Libby was actually off by her schedule but when Miss Gert had come in from the back and started gathering up salt and pepper shakers, Libby decided to help out. She poured the older woman a cup of coffee, grabbed a piece of cake and set it on the table in front of her, and told her to take a break while she filled the salt and pepper.

"Don't they carry rabies?" Libby knew they did but she didn't want to bluntly point that out.

Miss Gert had taken a bite of the lemon cake, so it was a moment before she answered but she was nodding her head. "Oh yeah, but this one doesn't act sick. In my limited experience, thank goodness, they walk crazy and look half dead. But maybe I need to get the vet to come out and see if she can get a look at it."

"That might be a good idea. Maybe you could set a trap and catch it."

"Might have to do that. So, how are you doing? Have you heard from Vance? I heard he won the bronc riding last night."

At the mention of Vance, she instantly remembered the night before he left. "He did. He called me." Not to brag about his win, but to check on her. He'd told her he'd won only when she'd asked him.

"I'm not one to pry, Libby. And I've done pretty good at it since you've been here. But is there anything I can do for you?"

Libby spilled salt on the table when she missed the opening of the salt shaker. Miss Gert had been a godsend to her. She'd helped her out, no questions asked. Libby took a deep breath. "I was driving in a rainstorm a little over two years ago and had a wreck." She told Miss Gert the story, even that she had been driving.

"Wow, you poor kid. Something like that can throw your world off its axel. Take some time to move forward. Is that what you struggle with?"

She rubbed her brow. "I struggle with the fact that I walked away barely hurt. And my husband, Mark, died. I blame myself. Living with that is hard, to say the least."

"Yeah, I get that. Have you told Vance this?"

She was assuming there was something between Libby and Vance. *Was it that apparent?*

"I have told him most of it. There are a few things I haven't told him. Or anyone." Things she could barely tell herself. Things she couldn't to this day wrap her mind around and accept. They were too painful.

"Would your husband want you half-living your

life, feeling guilty and unable to move on?"

Truth was, she wasn't sure what Mark would have wanted. Before that night, when they'd fought, she'd believed she'd known exactly how he thought, felt, and what he wanted out of life. She paused, twisting the cap of the shaker as her hand trembled. She couldn't think about that.

"Probably not." It was all she could say.

The door opened and Jenna, who had just come home from her honeymoon, came bursting inside, with her aunt Sally Ann following. "Wow, how did this happen? No one but you two here?"

"Hey, I'm back here," Hoss called through the opening above the grill. He was preparing cakes for tomorrow.

Libby had yet to offer to make pies. She wouldn't want to intrude on his space. But she was sure getting the hankering to bake some. *Maybe when Vance came home.*

"Sorry, Hoss. You have it smelling wonderful. Is that cake I smell?"

"Chocolate mud cake and I'm about to do an

Italian Cream"

"I don't know if I can resist that one. You bake the best Italian Cream cake I've ever tasted."

He grinned through the window. "It'll be ready in time for the dinner rush."

"So, you'll bake it, then Shep will come in for the evening shift and get all the credit?"

Hoss chuckled. "Long as I don't have to work the evening shift too often, I'm okay with that."

"Smart man," Jenna said. "Mind if I grab me and Sally Ann a couple of coffees?"

"I'll get them." Libby started to get up.

"Stay seated. I'm fine to serve myself."

"You know where it is." Gert grinned as Sally Ann pulled a chair from the table nearest to the booth and sank into it. "Busy day?" she asked her friend.

"We just had a van of about ten ladies come by. They were out of Austin and were making an all-day trip of antiquing/junkin'. All that work Jenna's been doing getting the word out about the store is sure bringing the business in. But goodness, I'm tired." She chuckled and took the mug of coffee Jenna handed her.

Jenna grabbed a chair and sat. "It's good for the bottom line and that's a great thing."

"I'm not complaining. I'm just a worn-out old gal." Sally Ann laughed then took a drink of coffee.

Hoss came out of the back, carrying three plates of lemon cake. Sally Ann's eyes brightened up at the sight of the cake. *Or was it the sight of Hoss?* Libby realized Sally Ann wasn't looking at the dessert.

"I thought you ladies might like a piece of my fresh lemon cake. You, too, Libby. You got Gert a piece earlier but not yourself."

"You are big and intimidating and as sweet as a cupcake." Jenna took the plate he offered her.

The big man very nearly blushed. Libby was fascinated. Sally Ann was still staring at him. Then she took the cake.

"Thank you. This might be exactly what I need to put some pep back in my step."

"Maybe," he said. "But I have to disagree with you. You're not a worn-out old gal."

Gert hitched a brow and looked up at her cook in surprise. Sally Ann blushed. Like red as the hot sauce on the table. And Jenna looked almost smug as if she'd already had suspicions these two might be sweet on each other. Libby thought about Hoss and the romance novels he'd confessed to reading…so maybe now she knew why. He was upping his game. The thought made her smile.

"Thank you. I think." Sally Ann looked awkward, holding a cup of coffee in one hand and the pie in the other as she looked up at Hoss.

He grinned. "Just thought I'd toss that out there. Enjoy." And then he walked back through the door to the kitchen, humming as he worked.

Sally Ann remained still.

Libby fought not to smile.

Gert cleared her throat. "You gonna sit there like a statue holding that coffee and cake or you gonna scoot to the table and enjoy it?"

Sally Ann set the coffee down then the cake and proceeded to scoot her chair to the table.

Jenna giggled and said quietly, "I think my sweet aunt has an admirer. I've suspected as much but now I'm certain."

"I do not." Her aunt took a bite of lemon cake.

Libby did the same, suddenly excited about the prospect of a little romance brewing with these two.

"I'm too old to have an admirer."

"You are not. Love is what makes the world go round."

Gert cough-laughed then continued in a whisper, "He gave her a piece of cake and now they're in love?"

"Who knows what can happen? I'm a newlywed, so I'm seeing love and roses for everyone right now. Speaking of which, Vance was completely smitten with you at the wedding." She had turned her bright eyes on Libby. "I hear the two of you are hitting it off with each other."

"I went to dinner at Beth and Cooper's place."

"And looked cozy with him in the goat pen, I hear."

Libby's stomach churned. "I fell. The goats are rambunctious."

"Very romantic." Jenna smiled. "I'm teasing but hopeful. I really like Shane's little brother. He's a sweetie."

Yes, he was. It seemed that everyone seemed to have the same consensus when it came to Vance.

"Beth and I are heading to Canton tomorrow. We're taking a trailer and planning on picking up some things for the shop. Aunt Sally Ann usually goes but she's sending me this time. I'm excited and thought you might want to come along. Girls' day out."

Libby was startled again. It was her day off. Kala, the waitress who worked only two days a week because of her small kids, was working the long shift tomorrow. Libby always felt odd taking a day off when Gert took time off very seldom. But she'd come to realize that Gert was happy when she stayed busy and insisted working kept her young.

"You should go. You'll have a great time," Gert urged.

"That would be fun," Libby agreed. Maybe it would keep her mind off Vance.

"Great. We're leaving about six so we can get there before ten."

"Sounds good to me."

"We might get you more involved in our little

155

town yet," Sally Ann said, finally sounding as if she were over her shock of Hoss's compliment.

Libby thought about that. The longer she stayed here, the more she thought about it as her home. Her heart was getting involved.

And it scared the daylights out of her.

It seemed that her life was perpetually about fear. *What had happened to the time when she'd lived each day with excitement? Guilt-free and happy?*

CHAPTER ELEVEN

Vance had never had two weeks move as slow as it had moved these last two. As he tugged on his gloves then started stretching to prepare for his ride, he knew he'd crossed a line. He had a national title to win and despite having won the last competition, his concentration had been off. It was off tonight.

"You okay?" his buddy, Clay Trelino, asked. He was up next and he slapped his hands on his thighs and lifted his arms to do one last stretch of his torso and shoulders before he would head to the chute.

"I'm fine. I'm just ready to get this over with and

head home."

Clay's lips hitched in a smile. "I can't get over you being stuck over a woman. You need to get your head in the game. You look ready to climb the walls. You need to concentrate or you're going to get hurt."

"I'm fine. Ride good and long out there," Vance said.

Clay bumped fists with him then strode to the platform to climb over the railing and lower himself onto the saddle bronc.

Vance continued stretching. Then, when the chute opened and Clay's ride bucked its way into the arena, he climbed the steps to the platform and watched. It was over in seconds and a good ride.

His name was called. He tugged his gloves one more time and headed toward the chute. *One ride and he was headed home.*

"Let's get this done," he muttered, then climbed over the railing. When the cowboy who was helping load everyone up nodded, he lowered himself onto the saddle.

He'd drawn the top ranked horse, which he was

glad of. He liked a challenge and felt like he was capable of riding any horse out there. He trained hard, worked on his strength, and kept in shape. Unlike many of his competitors, he watched his nutrition and trained like the athlete that he was. His confidence came from preparation, determination, and a God-given will to be the best he could be.

Yep, he was driven.

And right now, he rode hard and wild with only one thought on his mind: he would see Libby by tomorrow night if he loaded up as soon as the ride was over and he drove all night and day with as few stops as possible.

Libby had made it through the two weeks. She'd enjoyed her trip with Jenna and Beth to Canton. She had never seen so much stuff in one place at one time. There were vendors everywhere. Miles and miles of them. Jenna had given them the command to go forth and find cool things and make good deals. Libby had thought that was hilarious but she'd done her best and loved every moment. And she'd actually gotten several neat pieces for Miss Sally Ann's Junk Shop. They were hot and tired after the long day but after an eighteen-hour day, they made it home. But she'd come home with more than furniture for Jenna's aunt's store. She'd come home with two real friends.

And it had felt wonderful. They'd laughed and teased her about Vance. They'd laughed over messy but fantastic barbequed ribs. And eaten homemade peach ice cream from a local Texas grower.

They had helped her make it through the last week. But she'd talked to Vance and he would be home tomorrow. When she got off work at nine that evening, she hurried up the stairs and though she was tired, she was determined to have pies made for Vance. He'd baked for her; now she would welcome him home with her pies.

She had coconut cream bubbling on the stove and two crusts turning golden in the oven when the doorbell to the door at the bottom of the stairs rang. Glancing at her pie filling starting to thicken, she debated not answering. Then decided that wouldn't work. She turned the heat down, ran out the door and jogged down the stairs. She pushed the door open and froze.

A very tired, gorgeous Vance stood there, looking better than anything she'd ever seen.

"Vance," she gasped. Then, unable to stop herself, she threw her arms around his neck.

He instantly embraced her and snuggled his face against her neck. "I drove all night and day to get here to you," he said. "I know you have a lot on your mind but I can't help myself. I missed you. This was the longest two weeks of my life." He squeezed her closer. "You feel good."

She couldn't speak. She just knew that after all the worry and guilt she'd been through—and probably would continue to go through—this was the only place she wanted to be. *In Vance Presley's arms.* "I missed you so much."

He looked at her. Weariness etched his eyes. "I can't tell you how happy I am to hear that. Because I literally feel desperate to kiss you right now."

She smiled, feeling just as desperate. "Then

please, please kiss me."

His eyes sobered. "Are you sure? I mean, you have a lot to work through but I promise to help you any way I can. And to wait as long as you need me to."

She cupped his precious face. "I do have a lot. And I can't promise you that I'm not going to be on an emotional roller coaster sometimes. But I want to move forward. And I have some things to tell you."

His eye twinkled as he kissed the side of her neck. "Can you tell me later?"

"Yes," she squeaked.

Then he covered her lips with his, and Libby knew that in Vance she had found her light in the darkness.

Vance had longed for this moment from the moment Libby had dropped roast beef all over him. To know that she wanted to kiss him and had missed him as much as he missed her sent his heart soaring. She felt as though she belonged in his arms. And in his life. He wanted her in it more than he wanted to win the National Finals Rodeo title.

The fire alarm going off upstairs broke them apart. Libby yelped and started running up the stairs and he followed.

"What's going on?" he asked as smoke billowed down the stairs and the scent of something burning fill the air. "Hold on, Libby. Be careful."

"My pies!" Libby cried as she dashed through the door with him close behind her. There didn't seem to be any flames, so that was a relief as he watched her hurry to the stovetop.

"Oh yuck." She groaned and reached to turn off the electric burner; then, using a heat mitten, she lifted the pot off the hot surface.

He ran to the window and pushed it open then came to look over her shoulder. "Yum." It was an awful black, gooey gunk.

She giggled and it was a great sound to his ears.

"It's your coconut cream pie. It was almost ready when you rang my doorbell."

"Oh, so it's my fault." He laughed when she gave him a playful glare.

"I would say really bad timing. But I'm so glad

163

you're here that I'll make you a new pie."

"I do like the sound of that," he said over the fire alarm. "But I don't like the sound of that." He reached above the stove and twisted the fire alarm off its holder and was pulling out the battery when Libby gasped again.

"What?"

"My crust." She moaned and tugged open the oven door, where smoke poured out. She bent and a look of disgust swept across her face.

"Bad, huh?" He bent down to look at the crusts. They were black and crispy. He coughed. "Oh yeah," he drawled then chuckled.

She hit him on the arm with her mitten. "It is not funny."

"Oh yes it is." He took her mitten and then used it to reach for the first pie plate and pulled out the black crust, then the other. "I have to say, you did tell me you had a way with pies. And now I am a believer." Unable to help himself, he burst out laughing and then she did too. He swept her into his arms and swung her away from the stove. He flopped onto her love seat with her on his lap and smoke was swirling all around them. "Libby, darlin', I love you. I'm not rushing you but I just need you to know how I feel. I'm crazy about you."

She had one hand planted on his chest and she turned serious. "I have to tell you something."

"Whatever you need to."

"My name is Libby Dunaway, not Libby Smith. I lied when I first came to town because I was using cash and I didn't want anyone who might be looking for me to be able to find me. I sent the people who needed to know I was okay a text and told them I was fine, when I first ran. Then I bought a cheap, pay-as-you-go phone at a store so no one could track me. I just needed time alone. Time to figure things out. And so I just never came clean about my name."

Vance sat up straight. He hadn't thought about her using a fake name. "Okay. You did what you needed to do."

She moistened her lips. And hung her head for a moment. "I need to tell you about that night. The night of the wreck."

He could hear the angst in her voice and he smoothed her hair, trying to comfort her.

"It was my fault." She closed her eyes and worried the button on his shirt. He didn't even think she realized what she was doing. She opened her eyes and they were misty. "It was raining. And a really dark night. I was driving. I had picked my husband up from the airport. His job as a fire alarm consultant had him traveling some but when he was supposed to come home, he'd texted me that they needed him to stay until Monday, which meant he would spend the weekend there. So, on Monday, I picked him up and knew something was wrong the moment he got in the car."

Vance's gut twisted as he saw pain in her face. Her eyes dulled as if she had a terrible headache...but he knew it was heartache. He also knew something didn't feel right. But he let her talk and fought the desire to hold her close. He was still dazed, knowing she had missed him enough to sort through some of her feelings.

"I was driving. I could barely see in the rain. I

asked him what was wrong. He told me that he'd lied. And he told me he was so sorry, that he loved me and he always would but that he'd fallen in love with someone else." Her face tensed and his gut knotted with anger.

"What?" He could barely believe what she'd said. *How could someone not see what a treasure Libby was?*

"My reaction exactly. I took my eyes off the road and asked what? He said he was leaving me; he couldn't help it. That she'd come and spent the weekend with him, and he couldn't hurt her any longer."

"Hurt her, the mistress—but he could hurt you? What kind of man was he?" Vance growled.

Libby gave a defeated sigh. "I was in shock. I was looking at him, and the car swerved, caught the uneven shoulder and we spun out of control." Her voice was void of emotion. "When I woke up in the hospital, he was dead and I was alive. And I've been living a lie. I've been grieving the man I loved, the boy I fell for so long ago. And trying not to believe he was the person who got in the car with me that night. The man I killed. But I was beginning to know I needed to try to move forward. When I went to his grave a few months ago, his mistress found me there. We had a horrible confrontation and she told me I hadn't only killed the man she loved but the father of her little boy." Tears fell down her cheeks. "He was leaving me because she was pregnant, Vance. The pain of that and all the horrible memories of that night were too much. And I ran. And I've still been deceiving myself by sometimes pretending the infidelity never happened. What is wrong with me that I would do that?"

"I'm not sure, but it's probably a coping mechanism." He wasn't sure and thought she might need to see a therapist. This went deeper than he'd first thought. He tipped her chin so she looked at him. "You ended up here. And you're going to be all right. You were betrayed and hurt, and before you could adjust to the fact that the man you loved had done this to you, the wreck happened and he died. But you didn't kill him. That responsibility lies squarely on his shoulders."

"No. How was it his fault?"

"It was storming and he chose to break such cheap, scummy news to you while you were driving. What did he expect would happen? You were in shock and not functioning at full capacity when the car slid off the road. And that was his doing. Not yours, sugar."

Her expression faltered, as if comprehending what he was saying. Then her hand came up and covered her trembling lips. "I never thought of that. Never." She blinked hard, then her hands went to her cheeks. "I didn't kill him. And all this time…"

Leaning forward, she pressed her face in the crook of his neck and held onto him. "I feel as if a huge burden has been lifted from my shoulders."

"You should have never had the burden in the first place but I can see how you would take it, seeing how much you loved him."

Vance was torn. He needed to leave, to punch a tree or something. And he needed to stay and give Libby the support she needed. But realizing that she'd continued to grieve a man who had betrayed her that way showed him just how stuck on her deceased husband she was.

How could he compete with that?

He felt sick at heart.

"Look," he said. "I'm exhausted, and I need to get to the ranch and unload the horses. They've been in the trailer way too long. I'm going to go and give you some time to rest."

"Okay." She looked a little startled but stood so that he could stand.

He felt conflicted and he hated the anger and uncertainty flowing through him. And he hated the uncertainty in her eyes.

"Is everything okay?" she asked.

"Yes, just the trip has hit me." He pulled her into his arms and held her, absorbing the feel of her. "I better go." His emotions were mixed, confused.

She leaned back, but didn't let him go. "Are you sure everything is fine?"

"I'm fine. I'll be honest, though. I'm really struggling with how you mourned that jerk all this time. Even if it was a coping mechanism, I don't get it. What he did to you was about as low as it goes."

She paled a bit and he hated himself for hurting her. But he needed to be truthful; she finally was after all this time.

"I see," she said. "I don't understand it myself."

He cupped her cheek. "Maybe that's what you need to figure out before we go anywhere else in our relationship. This is way more than I suspected. I've got to go. I'll call."

And then he let her go, headed to the door, and jogged down the stairs.

CHAPTER TWELVE

The air was still filled with the scent of burned pie as Libby sank to the couch and stared at the empty doorway that Vance had just walked through. *Maybe out of her life.* She'd seen it in his eyes. The disbelief that she'd lived the last two years in denial about the truth of her marriage. She dropped her forehead into her palm and closed her eyes as she tried to make sense of her emotions and her reasoning.

She had been so betrayed by Mark. So very deceived and then, yes, it had been cruel—the way he'd come out and told her about his affair, his betrayal.

Why had she deceived herself all this time into not confronting the truth? *It hurt too much. It cut so deep.* It was true, but she could see how it didn't make sense to Vance.

Vance cared for her. Said he loved her… Joy and light filled her at the thought because she loved him too. She knew it now with a clarity that nothing could shake. But she had ruined their chances. And the fact was, could she really give her heart and her trust away again?

She looked around the small apartment and fought off tears. She had really gotten her life into a mess. She couldn't get over the look that had flashed in Vance's eyes when he realized what she was telling him. When it registered that she'd been having trouble moving on from Mark after what he'd done.

He covered his reaction up but then he'd pulled away and she knew he was struggling.

Looking at it from his point of view, she could see why he'd react that way. He had never loved someone and been betrayed. But for her, she hadn't had time to digest what had happened between them before he died.

Had she just not processed what had gone wrong in her marriage? Had she not looked deeper into what she'd done wrong that would make Mark do what he'd done? Her stomach dropped at the thought and it hurt to look deeper at this. *Was she to blame for the breakdown of her marriage, just like she was for Mark's death?*

Her heart raced, thinking about what she'd been struggling not to think about. The day she'd been confronted by Mark's mistress at the gravesite. These were the thoughts that had consumed her. She'd felt worthless while looking at the woman her husband had been planning to leave her for. And those feelings compounded now, as the darkness she'd been suppressing began to overtake her.

Vance was numb for two days since arriving home and finding out that Libby had been mourning this jerk she'd been married to all this time after what he'd done to her. And that she'd blamed herself for the wreck and Mark's death. His stomach was sick just thinking about it.

Thankfully, they had a Mustang sell happening that weekend and there was a lot to get done before the buyers and those adopting a horse would be here. He had as many horses to work with as he possibly could to make them calmer to better their chances for adoption. He'd buried himself in the breaking, working early morning and late into the night. He'd continually turned down offers of lunch at the café from his brothers. He'd also not talked to anyone about the problem he was so angry about.

And for three days, each of his brothers had remarked that Libby had seemed withdrawn as she'd worked the lunch crowd.

Vance hated that she might be hurting…but was she hurting because he'd walked away or was she hurting because she was still mourning the loss of the jerk who'd betrayed her and then chosen to tell her about it during a terrible rainstorm while she was driving? The man hadn't cared whether he put her in danger. *She could have been killed in that wreck instead of him.* The very thought sent chills raging through Vance and it was all he could do not to let the Mustang he was working with sense his anger.

"Are you going to take a break?" Cooper called, hanging his elbows over the arena railing and studying him. "You've been at this like a madman for three days."

"Yeah, take a break," Shane added, joining Cooper and Drake too.

Drake didn't say anything but Vance knew his oldest brother was thinking the same thing.

"I want to get as many horses ready for the sale as possible."

Shane stepped up on the bottom rung of the arena so he was more visible. "There's just two more days. You can't break them all before that and we all know they are going to need regular riding to get them properly acclimated in order to call them broke."

"Shane's right," Cooper said. "I'd be working with more but instead I'm riding the ones you've already broke to get them truly ready for adoption. Does this have to do with Libby? Did you two have a fight? We thought y'all were an item before you left."

It was all true but breaking them took more concentration from him and that was what he needed. He needed everything he could to take his mind off her. And still it wasn't enough. Libby was still there, troubling him in so many ways he couldn't process it all.

He loved her. He had hoped to make a life with her but he hadn't known the truth. Hadn't known she was still stuck on the man who had taken her life and her love so callously for granted.

"I'm fine," he bit out. "Okay, I'm fine. Libby, she's…" He clamped his lips together. *What could he tell them?* He had promised to keep her history to himself and now it was really backing him into a corner.

"Okay," Cooper said. "I can see there's some tension there and it's your business, brother. I'm going to go ride my ponies but I'm here if you need to talk."

"Same here," Shane said, sounding concerned but backing off.

He knew that if Brice wasn't transporting a load of cattle to Oklahoma, he'd have been right there with his brothers. They all knew that Vance had always processed his feelings while working with his horses and if he had pulled into himself, like now, then something was up. It had started early, as he'd told Libby, and it continued today. Horses gave him a safe place to think. But it wasn't working right now and his brothers' concern was only escalating his stress. His hands were tied. He had promised not to disclose Libby's past.

When Cooper and Shane strode away, he shot a glance back to the fence where Drake had pushed back his hat and continued to study him. Drake would press if he thought he needed to and Vance could see in his expression that he thought it was time.

"You going to give that horse a break and come look me in the eye and tell me what's up?"

"Nope," Vance quipped. This was his business and his big brother couldn't help, no matter how much Vance wanted a sounding board.

"If not for yourself, then for the Mustang. You and

I both know if that horse keeps sensing your tension, it's only going to make it more nervous. Give it a break."

Vance knew what he was saying was true. The black Mustang was overly nervous. "Whoa, boy," Vance said, calmly stepping back into the Mustang's sight. "It's okay."

He tied the horse to the arena fence, where the shade of the barn sheltered it. He would release it after it had time to relax. Vance turned back to Drake. "You're right."

Drake didn't say anything as Vance strode out of the gate and then over to where he waited.

"You and Libby obviously have something going on, and I don't want to pry, other than to tell you that I'm here. I know you can't talk but you look really down. Dad noticed it too."

Vance sighed, yanked his hat off and thumped it against his thigh. "I'm torn up, if you really want to know."

"I thought so. From what I could tell, she is too."

"That's not helping me. She did this."

Drake crossed his arms and his gaze narrowed. "Maybe she has too many problems for you to get involved with. You can't talk about them. But they're tearing you up."

Vance started walking and Drake fell into step with him. "That's what I'm deciding. But the problem is my heart is already involved."

"I know. Even if you hadn't told me as much the other day or again now, I would have known it. It's written on your face. You know, nothing you tell me will ever go anywhere else. If you need to talk, then I'm here."

"I know that and I appreciate it." Vance wondered whether he was being too hard on Libby. And he fought himself over whether to ask Drake for advice. "She's a widow. She hasn't let anyone know, as far as I'm aware of." Guilt slammed into him for revealing Libby's secret.

Drake stopped walking. "Wow, at her age— terrible."

"Yeah, my exact reaction. And it happened a little over two years ago, so she was even younger. She's struggling and even before that, she had a rough life. She's basically alone in the world. I'm not sure why she's not wanting anyone to know. I think she just needs a break from people around her feeling sorry for her. Or at least that was what I thought. Now, I'm not so sure."

"What's happened to alter your thinking on that?"

"She told me the night I got home that while she was driving in a rainstorm, her husband told her that he was leaving her, that he loved someone else. She hit a slick spot, went off the road and had a wreck, killing him. She was in the hospital, knocked out for a couple of days. And she's been mourning the creep. I thought she was mourning a good guy. The man she'd loved and lost. I could understand her struggling but this—this is not something I can understand."

Drake was silent. "This is rough," he said at last.

"Tell me about it. Am I crazy to be struggling with this? What was he thinking? She's been feeling guilty because she killed him. And there's more—his mistress was pregnant and blames her too. I'm not kidding you, Drake. And she's taken the blame for this instead of facing the truth."

"Okay, I get why you're so torn up. But, let's back up and breathe. There is no telling how all that could mess with a person's mind. And heart."

Vance felt like a heel. "I know. I hate myself right now but can't stop the anger tying me up."

"I get that. He could have caused her death instead of his."

"Exactly."

"You'd like to meet him in the parking lot and tear into him."

"Yeah, I would. And I understand she's suffered a traumatic event and loss. So why am I acting so irrationally?"

"I don't call you being irrational. You're angry. Just like when Mom died. Anger is okay, but you need to sort it out and get through it. And once you have, then, maybe you can see clearly. Give it some time. That's my advice. Sounds like she needs time too. But hopefully, at the end of the day, it works out for you both. But Vance, you might not be able to get past knowing her feelings for the guy are that strong. And she might not be able to get past it. I'm no doctor but that's what my gut tells me."

Drake had always had a great gut and it was usually right. Vance let his words sink in.

"I think I'll walk. And then come back and finish working the horse. I hate not keeping her confidence but I needed help."

"It goes nowhere." Drake nodded as emphasis that his word was his bond.

Vance had a moment of guilt over betraying his word to Libby. But in this instance, he truly felt getting his brother's input was helpful to him, considering his own thoughts might be too influenced by the emotions of anger toward Libby's dead husband.

"I know." He held Drake's gaze. "That's the only reason I let you in. Thanks."

CHAPTER THIRTEEN

Libby was getting off on Saturday afternoon and about to head up to her apartment, where she planned to decide what her next move was. Vance hadn't been into town or called since the night she'd revealed the truth to him. She'd done endless hours of thinking and she'd shed tears, not for Mark but for the loss of Vance.

How had she been so blind? Her heart had ached for what she and Mark had had, or what she'd believed they'd had and he'd destroyed. And like Vance had pointed out, because of Mark's careless timing on delivering his life-changing punch to her heart, he endangered her life and she could have been killed rather than him. He'd had no right to do what he'd done. None of it. He'd made bad choices and she'd had to live with the consequences. But she'd betrayed Vance's trust and he'd obviously decided she had gone too far. So, maybe it really was time to move on. She had saved enough money to buy an old car...a very cheap clunker but it would run. The mechanic in town had salvaged it and had it for sale. It was her ticket out of town.

As she pulled open her door, Beth pulled up in front of her apartment. "Hey, are you off for the day?"

Beth had been super to her, and Libby was going to miss her and Jenna, and also Bella and Lori. They'd all befriended her and brought her into the fold when she'd needed it so much.

"I am. I'm about to chill on the couch with my feet up. What's up?" She knew that today was the Mustang sell and adoption out at the ranch. She'd thought for two weeks that she'd be out there, watching the process. But she didn't belong out there anymore.

"Well, me and the girls, we're setting up the buffet, getting ready for the big shindig at the ranch and we figured since you and Vance had had this spat, or whatever it is that's happened between you two, that you were probably not going to come out there. So I came to haul you out there."

"Thanks, but no. I don't need to be there."

Beth stuffed her hands on her hips. "Yes, you do. He is miserable. Cooper said he's never seen him like this. Not as an adult. Not since he was younger and had internalized his grief over their mother's death. He told me that Vance always, always disappeared into his horses when he was troubled. But he's really worried about him. And I'm worried about you."

Libby's heart clenched tight and her stomach twisted at the thought of Vance being in pain because of her. He had been so good to her. If she'd just leveled with him...if she'd just leveled with herself, maybe they'd have had a chance and he wouldn't have had to be so hurt.

"I know something is wrong. You've been

different. More like you were when you first came to town. You had gotten better and started opening up but now, can you talk about it? Would it help to have someone listen?"

"Do you have time to come up for a few minutes?"

Beth smiled. "I have all the time in the world."

Libby didn't say anything; she just opened her door and led the way up the stairs. She took a stool at the small kitchen bar that was used as the kitchen table. Beth took the other one and she told her friend what she'd done.

"So, you have been blaming yourself for Mark's death all this time. Wow. And the guy betrayed you like that."

Libby nodded slowly, seeing the shock in Beth's expression as she learned the truth and the whole story. It was so clear to Libby now that she'd been living in denial. "And Vance just couldn't take that I'd mourned Mark all this time after what he'd done to me. He saw the timing as one more thing Mark did to show how he cared nothing about my feelings and to Vance, that was the last straw for him, thinking I could mourn a man after that deep a betrayal."

"I get it. I see exactly what he must be feeling."

"Mark made terrible decisions. And needless to say, my marriage wasn't what I thought it was. I have been in denial and the truth hurt too badly, I think, for me to face. Now I don't know what I'm going to do. I've hurt the man who helped me so much. The man..."

"You've fallen in love with?" Beth smiled gently.

Libby nodded.

Beth reached out and took her hands. "Stop running. Stop living in denial. You have the opportunity to make decisions for your life right now. I hope you make the right ones."

Libby's heart ached deeper and every cell in her body said run. Running was easier than facing the hard stuff. But somewhere down the road, she'd given in to going the easier route.

Could she stick? Could she at least face Vance,

even if she saw his disbelief and distrust of her shining in those beautiful green eyes she loved so much?

The adoption was in full swing and thankfully was keeping Vance busy. The turnout was amazing. They'd never had a turnout like this one. So many people had come to help the wild Mustangs, wanting to give one a home. Wanting to give twenty a home. People with varying space were committed to adopting and some committed to buying in order to help the cause by buying a horse so that the money could be used to feed and board another group of Mustangs their ranch would get as soon as space permitted.

His job, like Cooper and Brice and Shane's, was to ride the Mustangs to show the horses' varying degrees of saddle readiness. They had several round pens set up inside the large round pen, enabling them to show several at the same time.

Vance was riding in the center pen. And despite how much he cared for the horses, his heart wasn't in it today. He wasn't sleeping, wasn't eating. And he knew that he had to make a decision. He couldn't go on like this. It wasn't fair to him and it wasn't fair to Libby.

What must she be thinking?

He had just dismounted and was signing the adoption slip for the family who wanted the horse he'd just ridden for them. "Take that to the man at the front table, my brother Drake, and he'll get you all the necessary paperwork. Thank you. This little pony will be a great horse for you and your family."

"Thanks." The cowboy shook his hand then led his daughter and wife away.

"Vance."

He stiffened, knowing it was Libby behind him. His stomach went bottoms up as he turned. She was pale and drawn and it hurt him to see her like that. "Libby." He cleared the lump from his throat.

"Can you take a break?"

He looked around and nodded. He needed to talk to her. To explain why he reacted the way he had. "Sure. I think that's a good idea."

He undid the chain holding the temporary round pen closed and moved to the outside of the bars and then closed it back. He glanced around and caught his brothers watching. "Let's go out of the covered arena area where it's quieter."

He led her past the entrance, where Drake and his dad looked up and nodded at him with support. He led her past the buffet tent, where he could see all the ladies watching. He felt like a fish in a fishbowl suddenly.

"Maybe we'll go to the backyard. No one should be there and my mom's swing is there. It'll be quiet."

She nodded and walked with him across the parking lot and around the house to the tree-shaded side yard where the porch swing, well varnished and maintained all these years later, sat overlooking a pond in the center of the pasture.

"Please sit." He waited until Libby sat and then he sat beside her.

"I'm sorry," she said.

"No need to be sorry," he offered. "I judged you and it wasn't my place."

Her eyes flashed. "Yes, it was. I didn't tell you the truth when I should have." She blinked sudden tears. "I hurt you and that was the last thing I wanted to do. But you were right. I have lived a lie for two years. I couldn't face the truth. It hurt too much and maybe it made me question myself, and what I might have done wrong. Maybe I was living in denial prior to that fateful night when everything fell apart. I really don't know."

"I'm sorry, Libby. I have been angry when I just couldn't justify you being so hurt and accepting it with the mourning. I should have been more open but I love you and can't stand the thought of what he did to you."

Her hand had gone to her mouth and she blinked rapidly. "Wait, let me finish. Mark made some terrible decisions and well, I have too. But, in the end, you pointed out that those decisions brought me here. And that is the best thing that has ever happened to me. I was about to make the decision to leave and Beth showed up. I told her the truth and she asked me to come here to face this. To not run again. You said you loved me. Do you still? Because I love you. And I never thought I could give my heart again, but I have and if you could just look past how mixed up I was and give me another chance…"

Vance took her hands, his heart swelling. "Libby, darlin', I love you. I was wrong not coming back and getting this sorted out before now. I want you in my life. I need you in my life and I promise my heart is yours and will always be yours. If you want me."

"Oh Vance, I want you. I need you so much. I thought I had lost you. And nothing in my life has ever, ever hurt so much."

He closed his eyes as her words sank in. When he opened his eyes, he smiled from his heart and reached for her. She came willingly and he pulled her onto his lap and held her so close, breathing in her scent, her feel and just thanking God that they'd found each other.

"I need to ask you something." He gently kissed her lips. Wanting to linger, to deepen the kiss, wanting to kiss her forever. "Will you marry me? Is it too soon to ask—"

"Yes. I mean, no, it's not too soon to ask. And yes, I'll marry you." She laughed, breathless as she cupped his face and kissed him soundly. "I wasn't leaving until you asked me. At least I was hoping you would."

He smiled against her onslaught of kisses. "I hoped you would forgive me."

"No forgiveness needed. This was hard but I can see clearly now. So clearly my future with you. Here on this ranch and in this town. My place is with you."

"And my place is with you." He breathed against her lips and then he kissed her with the emotion and the passion and gratefulness that overflowed him for this special woman.

And sitting there on the swing his mother loved, he felt her smile…and he knew from here, his future with Libby would bloom.

Excerpt from

DRAKE: THE COWBOY AND MAISY LOVE

Cowboys of Ransom Creek, Book Six

CHAPTER ONE

Maisy Love's gut told her something was wrong, and her gut was usually right.

Driving her Jeep down the deserted country road, pulling her small travel trailer behind her, she hoped this time it was wrong. She was in the boonies, the middle of nowhere because she'd decided on the spur of the moment to detour. Yep, that same gut had said go for it and she had altered her course from her Texas

Hill Country destination and taken a side trip down a stretch of road she'd not explored before. She was now skirting the hill country area very much off the beaten track.

Been here done this before, if it wasn't for her stinkin' gut churning now, she'd still be excited at the prospect of finding a few new diners appropriate for her food blog and live video channel. Sometimes the best places were discovered by accident. Or detours.

The Jeep jerked and made a weird noise. Her heart lurched in surprise and she pressed the brake and got the Jeep to the side of the road. Drat her gut, right again.

Breathing a sigh of relief that the wheels were not rolling any longer she put the Jeep in park and turned it off just as another weird noise came from somewhere beneath her or behind her. Was it the Jeep or the trailer?

She opened the door, jumped out and bent down to look under the Jeep and the travel trailer.

"Oh no," she gasped. There was a piece she was pretty sure wasn't supposed to dangle down under the trailer. This was not good.

Not good at all.

Still, on her knees, she looked down the deserted road and ran through her options. She really only had one: call for help, because she certainly had no idea how to fix whatever it was that was wrong. Of course, traveling state to state, pulling her home behind her as she interviewed small-town café owners across the country for her internet show, On The Road with Maisy Love, exposed her to all sorts of new adventures. She loved her career. Though it was a one-woman show, she was able to support her travel habit with the income she made from ads and merchandise she sold in her Maisy Love store. It was a dream come true. She'd just recently sent an email with a video clip, taking a long shot at getting a spot on a cooking competition on the Food Network. The idea of actually competing against other foodies was a little nerve-racking but it would be great exposure.

And right now, though she was doing okay financially, some extra exposure to help bring in some extra money for emergency repairs like this was greatly needed. She pulled her phone from her pocket and made the road service call. Thankfully she'd paid the extra fee to AAA that enabled towing for a hundred miles or so and there just happened to be a small town called Ransom Creek not too far down the road.

While she waited for the tow truck, she pulled the small ranching town up on her phone app and was relieved to see that it sounded like a great place to check out while repairs were being made, if they had a mechanic. Another quick search showed that yes they had one but only one. They also showed a café for her to check out, the Goodnight Café. She loved the name and hoped the food and the owner lived up to the cute name. If so, Maisy may have just found her next show.

Forever the optimist she was smiling when the rust covered wrecker came to her rescue.

Drake Presley was a cowboy, *not* a skunk wrangler.

Still, here he stood, hidin' out on the back porch of the Goodnight Café in wait for a stinking polecat that had been showing up behind the café off and on for the last month. It was good at avoiding the cage traps but needed to be caught. It had almost sprayed Gert twice when she'd gone out to her storage building before she'd asked for help. And this morning she'd twisted her ankle running up the steps, getting away from the critter. Thankfully, she hadn't gotten sprayed, but she was going to be hurting for a few days.

He wasn't going to let her get hurt again. He was going to trap him a skunk and haul it off to the woods away from people.

Shifting his weight from one leg to the other as impatience welled within him, he peeked toward the shed, looking from his hiding place against the back wall of the diner's porch. He studied the shed and the surrounding vacant lots stretching out from it toward the old gas station, turned repair shop, that set down the road.

Nothing. His brows dipped. If ever there was a sneaky skunk, this was it. They'd set traps, and it had somehow managed to not enter the cage.

His phone buzzed in his pocket. He slipped it out and saw his brother, Brice's, name on the ID. "What?"

he hissed in a barely audible sound.

"You sound weird."

"I'm standing here trying to surprise a skunk that's probably going to shoot me with both his spray guns before I catch him. How do you think I'm supposed to sound?"

Brice chuckled. "Right, so, no luck?"

"Not yet," he growled, scanning the area. "Did you need something in particular?"

"Just checking on you. I went by the hospital and checked on Gert. She's going to be off her feet for a week or so."

"I was afraid of that."

"Do you need help? I'll bring reinforcements."

"Thanks, but I've got this."

There was a pause. "I've heard that before but it was worth a try."

When they were kids, after his mother died while in childbirth with their little sister, Lana, Drake had been the oldest and had instantly taken on the role as his dad's helper. And he'd always tried to handle everything himself. Those years had been hard, just from the loss of his mother and the horrible adjustments the family had had to make during that time. But he'd not helped matters sometimes because he'd taken his role so seriously. They all knew now that that had been his way of coping. But it hadn't been easy and he still, sometimes tried to take care of everything instead of asking for help.

"No need for both of us to possibly get sprayed—" he halted mid-sentence when he heard something. "Hey, gotta go. I think it's game time."

"Good luck and don't get sprayed…"

Drake hung up as his brother's chuckles rang from the phone.

Maisy walked from the repair shop toward the diner. Lenny, the mechanic told her it would take a few days to get her antique Jeep fixed. Then he'd told her where the diner was and suggested she go there for some lunch and figure things out. He'd told her about a nice bed-and-breakfast down the street from the diner and said that she should go there and get Sally Ann to set her up for a few days. Most people would be stressed about this news, but Maisy glanced around and felt optimistic about her whole adventure.

She could dig spending a few days here. Especially if the café was as good as he'd said. She wasn't sure how much trust to put in the little man's description of the food, not when he had looked as if he'd give a greasy burger a five-star rating, but considering this looked like maybe her only option, she was hoping every rave review he'd given the owner Gert Goodnight and her Goodnight Café was as deserving as he stated. She loved hitting the off-beaten track and finding fun new places; she had high hopes as she took the shortcut across the vacant lot behind the garage and the back of the diner. She had walked parallel to the buildings lining up beside the diner and now stepped out into the field in order to turn the corner to head up the small alley that he'd said led to the front of the café. It was at that moment she spotted the black-and-white cat. She loved cats, and they loved her.

"Hey, little kitty." She stepped forward toward the

scraggly bush not too far from the porch. She bent down to get a better look at the cat, to coax it out so she could pet it. Black beady eyes blinked at her from beneath the bush…she froze and swallowed hard as her eyes caught the white stripe running from between those eyes and running the length of the black skunk. "A, a skunk."

"Straighten up slowly," a very masculine voice instructed her from somewhere to her left.

She had no options and was grateful for instructions because she had never been practically nose-to-nose with a stinky skunk before and had no clue what her options were. *Maybe if she ran, it could catch her like a bear would do. Could skunks run that fast?*

Her heart thundered as she swallowed her fear and desire to make a dash for it. Instead, she slowly straightened up and out of the corner of her eye, she saw a cowboy—*oh goodness, what a cowboy*. He stepped slowly off the porch. Her gaze darted to him and for a moment she forgot why she was standing frozen like an icicle behind the café.

He was tall, had black hair, tanned skin made even darker by the crisp white cotton shirt he wore with well-worn, starched jeans that ended at shiny buffed boots the color of rich mahogany. But that wasn't what stole her mind. It was the vibrant green eyes that bore into her with serious intent, mesmerizing her, or hypnotizing her to do as he said. Right now, she'd do just about anything he told her to do, even if there wasn't a skunk at her feet.

Skunk at my feet. Her gaze shifted at lightning speed to the beady-eyed creature glaring up at her. She flinched, knowing in that instant she was done. In a quick flick, its tail shot up and the little beast hopped around and aimed—

In that same instant, strong hands grasped her around the waist as the handsome cowboy yanked her close to his rock-hard body and swung them around so he shielded her from the stout rank scent that exploded from back of the awful black-and-white fluffball.

The scent filled the air. Maisy covered her nose while at the same time completely aware that she was being shielded by the cowboy. *What a nice guy.*

Amazing, really, that he'd done something so nice. Then again there was probably no way she was walking away from this smelling like a rose. Nope, a toilet maybe, but no rose.

But him...oh dear goodness, he stunk, and he stunk bad.

"I told you not to move," he growled into her ear, his breath warm against her skin.

"I didn't," she bit back as the shock of what had just happened settled over her like the scent seeping into their pores.

Without another comment, he swung her into his arms; she gasped as he strode forward, away from the nasty scent that hovered in the air. He didn't stop until they were around the corner of the diner in the alley that she'd been headed to when she'd been distracted by the skunk.

"What in tarnation were you thinking in the first place when you went after that skunk?" he demanded in a not-so-very-nice tone.

"I thought it was a cat."

"Well, clearly you need to have your eyes

checked."

They had come around the corner but they were not smelling any better considering the scent had followed them. Her eyes were burning and her nose had started to burn too.

"It was black and white. It was an easy mistake."

"If you say so. I had been waiting for that blamed skunk all morning. Your mistake cost me, in more ways than one." He set her on her feet and stuffed his hands on his hips as he glared down at her. His very nice nose crinkled in defense of the scent. "This is bad."

"Yes, it is." She stepped back from him, testing the possibility that she might not smell as horribly as he did. Feeling guilty at the same time that he had taken the brunt of the hit. Her own nose crinkled as if trying to shrink away from the smell too. She wrapped a hand around the back of her neck and rubbed the tight muscles. "What are we going to do?"

"I think we need to get this stink off of us."

"How? It's awful, will it come off?"

His lip twitched, and he almost smiled. "Lots of

tomato sauce is in our futures. Although, I have to say it didn't help all that much when I was a kid and this happened."

The very thought this wasn't coming off was horrifying. The smell seemed to be intensifying. "But, I don't have a place to do that. My ride and my travel trailer are at the repair place being fixed. I was going to check into a bed-and-breakfast after I ate."

His brows dipped over his serious eyes. "Well, then, I guess we head down to Sally Ann's place. Maybe she can get you the room on the back of the bed-and-breakfast so you don't run all her other guests off."

That would be terrible. "I wouldn't want to do that." She was about to show up and possibly get turned away because she could run off the poor woman's other patrons. *What would she do? Go back to her travel trailer and take a shower while it was being repaired?* "This is not good."

His nose crinkled, making the handsome features relax slightly. "Tell me about it. But Sally Ann can help, or I can call in the cavalry. You'll be okay. I'm

Drake Presley, by the way."

"I'm Maisy Love."

"That's really your last name?"

"That's really my last name."

"I guess that's not so bad for a woman but I'd hate to be a man with a moniker like that."

She laughed. "I see your point." There were a lot of other names out there that could be worse, but she didn't point that out. "Who is the cavalry?"

"My family. We'll take care of you." He started walking down the alley toward the front of the diner and she followed him. The man had a walk that was decisive, long strides and with purpose. As if he'd made a decision and now he was implementing it and nothing better get in his way. She followed him, pretty certain herself that she didn't want to get left behind, standing on the sidewalk of the main road with people looking at her and wondering why she smelled so horrible. That would be humiliating.

There were cars and trucks pulled into the slanted parking spaces that lined the street. The diner, or café since that was what was on the sign, looked busy this morning. There were a few people coming out of the place as they rounded the corner. A couple of cowboys laughed as they talked about something. The moment they saw them, they stopped talking and their gazes locked on them. Surprise registered on their handsome faces and they took a step back.

"Drake, what in the world? Did you tangle with a polecat?" The surprise turned to a grin and the cowboy's eyes twinkled with laughter as he swiped his hat from his head and fanned it toward them to ward off the scent permeating from them.

"I think it's obvious I did." He frowned. His gaze shifted to her, and she thought she saw apology in their beautiful depths. "Fella's this is Maisy Love. And Maisy, these are my brothers, Shane and Cooper, pay no attention to him." He indicated Cooper with a sharp nod.

Cooper's eyes lit with devilish mirth. "I couldn't help but tease my older brother. He's a little uptight, if you haven't noticed. And normally he knows how to avoid skunk spray so I'm curious about how or what distracted him."

"That's my fault. He was trying to keep it off of me. I'm afraid I'm the one who didn't see it coming." She grimaced and hated that she'd caused this. She caught Drakes jaw tense and his gaze narrow as it drilled into Cooper. She was more intrigued but also felt bad.

"Not a problem. He'll live," Shane said, eyeing her with concern. "That's pretty bad, though. It's going to be rough getting rid of that scent."

"Tell us about it. And I'm not sure that's going to do the job." Drake frowned. He reached a hand out and cupped her elbow. "We're heading to Sally Ann's and see if she has a place for Maisy, maybe at the back so she doesn't disturb the other guests."

"Jenna is there. They'll fix her up. You'll be in good hands."

Maisy hoped so. She was starting to feel nauseous. The scent was starting to overpower her instead of her getting used to it. And he had her worrying that they might not be able to get rid of it. "We better go before we both pass out from the smell."

"Yeah, y'all might need to get that off as quick as

possible. How about me and Shane go to the store and pick up some more supplies?" Cooper asked, grimacing while his eyes crinkled at the edges.

Drake's nose twitched. "That'd be great. Get a lot. Enough for me and for Maisy. I don't have any in my cabinets. And stop grinning."

"I'm not grinning."

"Your eyes are about to tear up you're holding back so much laughter."

Cooper laughed. "Okay, so I can't help myself. But I'm on my way to your rescue. I'll run yours by your house and Shane can bring Maisy's by the B&B."

"Sounds like a plan."

She was relieved. It sounded as though she might get this gone soon. There would be no interviewing at the Goodnight Café until she didn't smell like a garbage dump.

Drake was quiet as he took Maisy to the B&B. He wondered about her but didn't ask questions. He could tell by the fact that she was starting to turn a tinge of green that she needed to have this skunk scent off her and soon. When they arrived at Sally Ann's, both women were waiting on the porch. He knew immediately that Shane had called his wife, Jenna, and told her what was coming. He wondered who was watching their store across the street.

Sally Ann's grin was as bright as a high-powered spotlight as she watched them walk up the steps to the yellow house with the colorful porch furniture. Jenna was smiling too and there was a teasing twinkle in her eyes.

"Whew, you two sure know how to make an entrance. Drake, what'd you do to this poor girl?" The junk store and B&B owner fanned the air in front of her face, her nose crinkled.

"We found Gert's skunk," Drake said, in no mood to tease.

"Did you get it?"

He frowned and his gaze shifted automatically to Maisy. "Nope. It got away."

Maisy's pale-eyes had a lavender hue, and they flashed a deeper shade as she turned rose. "That would be my fault." Exasperation rang in her tone.

"There will be another chance." Jenna glared at Drake. "I'm sure my brother-in-law won't let a little skunk get the better of him."

"I'll get it. But first, we have to get rid of the stench it gifted us with. Sally Ann and Jenna, this is Maisy Love. She walked up on the skunk while I was about to trap it."

"And it sprayed you both?" Jenna looked sympathetic while starting to fan the air in front of her nose too.

"No, he tried to protect me and took most of the hit." Maisy looked embarrassed, and he felt bad for her while something in his chest tightened. "I was on the way from the repair shop to the diner and then I was going to come here and get a room if you have one. I met the skunk instead. I thought it was a cat."

Sally Ann and Jenna both looked baffled at her words. He understood their look. Despite the irritating fact that she'd caused all of this, he felt bad for her having been sprayed. But, the fact that she was clueless about the difference in a black-and-white cat and a black-and-white skunk…well, he'd ignore that because he couldn't fathom how anyone could make that mistake. Obviously, Sally Ann and Jenna were having the same struggle.

"I'm not a country girl. I've never seen a skunk up close," she said, as if realizing what they were all thinking. "Anyway, do you have a room? Can you help me? If not, I guess I'll have to get some tomato sauce and find a creek somewhere."

"Of course, we're going to help you," both ladies said at the same time.

"But tomato sauce is just a myth. It takes baking soda, peroxide, and dishwashing detergent to get it off skin and animals. I've got enough to fix you up, but just in case, they're bringing backup."

"I'm glad you know what to do," Maisy said. "We don't have to pretend to be spaghetti." She smiled brightly at him.

Those teasing eyes tempted him.

"Good to know. Thank you, ladies. I'm heading out." Drake tipped his hat at Sally Ann, then met Maisy's gaze before he headed back the way he'd come.

He couldn't get out of there fast enough.

More Books by Debra Clopton

Turner Creek Ranch Series

Treasure Me, Cowboy (Book 1)

Rescue Me, Cowboy (Book 2)

Complete Me, Cowboy (Book 3)

Sweet Talk Me, Cowboy (Book 4)

New Horizon Ranch Series

Her Texas Cowboy (Book 1)

Rafe (Book 2)

Chase (Book 3)

Ty (Book 4)

Dalton (Book 5)

Treb (Book 6)

Maddie's Secret Baby (Book 7)

Austin (Book 8)

Cowboys of Ransom Creek

Her Cowboy Hero (Book 1)

The Cowboy's Bride for Hire (Book 2)

Cooper: Charmed by the Cowboy (Book 3)

Shane: The Cowboy's Junk-Store Princess (Book 4)

Vance: Her Second-Chance Cowboy (Book 5)

Drake: The Cowboy and Maisy Love (Book 6)

Brice: Not Quite Looking for a Family (Book 7)

About the Author

Bestselling author Debra Clopton has sold over 2.5 million books. Her book OPERATION: MARRIED BY CHRISTMAS has been optioned for an ABC Family Movie. Debra is known for her contemporary, western romances, Texas cowboys and feisty heroines. Sweet romance and humor are always intertwined to make readers smile. A sixth generation Texan she lives with her husband on a ranch deep in the heart of Texas. She loves being contacted by readers.

Visit Debra's website at www.debraclopton.com

Sign up for Debra's newsletter at
www.debraclopton.com/contest/

Check out her Facebook at
www.facebook.com/debra.clopton.5

Follow her on Twitter at @debraclopton

Contact her at debraclopton@ymail.com

If you enjoyed reading *Vance: Her Second-Chance Cowboy* I would appreciate it if you would help others enjoy this book, too.

Recommend it. Please help other readers find this book by recommending it to friends, reader's groups and discussion boards.

Review it. Please tell other readers why you liked this book by reviewing it on the retail site you purchased it from or Goodreads. If you do write a review, please send an email to debraclopton@ymail.com so I can thank you with a personal email. Or visit me at: www.debraclopton.com.